A Flag in the Window

Dear Pat,

I'm thrilled that you want to read my book. I hope you like it!

Best wishes always,

By

Brian "2012"

Brian Karadashian

Nov. 20, 2014

Dear Jason,

This is a book written by a friend of mine. He and I were teachers in the same elementary school in Poway. I pass it on to you to read and enjoy a story of a boy in 1943. Love,

Grandma Pat "2014"

First published by Dog Ear Publishing
4010 W. 86th Street, Ste H
Indianapolis, IN 46268
www.dogearpublishing.net

ISBN: 978-1-4575-1603-0

This book is printed on acid-free paper.

Printed in the United States of America

for Marcia and Samantha

Foreword

I am honored to have been asked to paint the cover for Brian Karadashian's children's historical novel *A Flag in the Window*, a book which evokes the spirit of homefront America as well as any I have ever read.

The story depicts a year in the life of twelve-year-old Billy Roarke, whose father is a paratrooper stationed in England. Karadashian's book is firmly rooted in 1943; he does a fine job of describing that era with more than just the standard images of the time: the swing music, the war bond posters, etc. He transports the reader with the language, along with the appropriate sensibilities, of the period. Young readers of *A Flag in the Window* will learn how people spoke then, but more importantly, what they thought and how they thought. Karadashian nicely captures the *zeitgeist* of 40s America.

But this book is more than that. *A Flag in the Window* transcends eras, like all good literature does, by illuminating humanity. One example: Billy's friend Mac, a soda jerk at the local pharmacy, reluctantly conveys the horrors of war he experienced in the trenches during the Great War. Of the hundreds of books I have read on World War I, I have never read such a moving and insightful depiction of friendship amidst the horrors of trench warfare. The scene is short and simple, as is the book, but powerful, as is the book.

This story is ultimately about redemption, and the dramatic twists and turns the story takes to arrive at that redemption make this book entertaining and compelling, to the point that I believe it would make a fine motion picture.

A Flag in the Window is a fine — and unique — children's book, and, to my mind, it deserves to become a classic of American homefront literature.

Richard DeRosset

One

Billy Roarke ran down the street, hoping he wasn't too late. He slammed into a wooden newsstand, nearly knocking a cigar from the face of the man seated behind the counter.

"Hey, what's the big idea?"

"Sorry, mister," Billy said. "You got any late editions?"

"Yeah, I got late editions. Here." The man slapped a *Los Angeles Times* newspaper in front of Billy as if he were swatting a fly. The twelve-year-old boy thanked the man, placed a nickel on the counter and took the paper.

Billy sat on the curb lining downtown Pasadena's Colorado Boulevard and scanned the front page of the paper, dated Monday, October 4, 1943. He read the article under the headline, "New Italy Area Taken," and then returned the newspaper to its fold.

Rising from the curb, his eyes found a figure known to him. His friend and classmate Randall Hill approached Billy, holding a bag of groceries in one arm.

"Hey, Randall."

Randall gave him a gentle punch on the arm with his free hand. "What's doin', Billy?"

"Aw nothin'. Just got a . . ."

"Hey," Randall interrupted, "guess who I just saw at the butcher shop? Thomas, that kraut kid in our class. That kid's a full-blooded German. No foolin'. Ain't got no American in 'im at all."

"Yeah?"

"Yeah. Hey, we shouldn't let them full-blooded ones stay in this country. And his old man ain't in the war. It makes me kind o' suspicious, ya know? Maybe they're spies or somethin'."

Billy lifted and dropped his shoulders. "What can we do about it?"

"We can rough him up a bit, ya know? I'm gonna find out tomorrow at school how come his old man ain't in the war."

"I don't think we should rough him up, but you're right. That sounds awful suspicious. Hey, you wanna get a soda? My treat."

"Nah. Can't. My old lady'll belt me good if I'm late with this stuff. I gotta go. So long, Billy." Randall put two hands under the bag and left for home.

Billy walked up the street to Himmelfarb's Pharmacy and Soda Fountain. A "Back the Attack – Buy War Bonds" poster was taped to the front window.

A cluster of tiny bells, dangling from the top of the glass door, sang his arrival as he entered the store. The smell of vanilla greeted him, along with the smooth swing sound of the Glenn Miller Orchestra playing on the radio situated behind the soda fountain counter where he took a seat.

A smiling man in a white apron, T-shirt and two-cornered hat approached him. "Hiya, Billy. What's the good word?"

"Hi, Mac."

"What'll it be today, my friend?"

"You got any chocolate?"

"Have I got chocolate? Get a load o' this." Mac lifted a large can of chocolate powder from a low shelf under the counter. "I take good care of my favorite war correspondent. Chocolate soda?"

"Yes, please."

"You got it, pal."

Mac turned and reached for a thick and heavy soda glass. He filled the narrowed bottom with chocolate powder, then sprayed soda water into the glass. The piercing sound of the water leaving the seltzer bottle overwhelmed Glenn Miller and his band, but the sound was music to Billy's ears. Mac left room for two scoops of vanilla ice cream, then handed his creation, stabbed with a straw and a spoon, to his delighted customer.

Billy took a long drink, knowing that the initial taste of something good is always the best, and fully savored his first taste of chocolate in a long time. "Boy, that's good. Thanks."

"You betcha. So, what's goin' on in the war, my friend? Gimme the lowdown."

"The Allies are really movin' through Italy, all right. I heard on the radio that General Eisenhower said we should be in Rome by the end of the month."

"That's beautiful. We're rollin' now. And, we got great people like your pop fightin' for us. He's a pilot or somethin', ain't he, your dad?"

"He's an engineer with the paratroopers," he said through a mouthful of ice cream. "He's in England."

3

"Beautiful. One of the smart guys. We need smart guys to win a war. And, we need guys like me. You know, I went down to sign up the day after Pearl Harbor. Yessir, Monday mornin' I went right down there at 8:00 sharp, sayin', 'Sign me up; I'm ready to go.' They didn't take me; says I was too old. Too old? Hah. I'm forty-five years old and I'm strong. I was in the Great War and I know how to fight. I know how to fight better'n these young pups they're sendin' out there." Mac raised his arms in resignation. "But, what are ya gonna do? They sent me home and here I am."

Billy mined his soda for another clump of ice cream. "I think the war'll end soon, though. Don't you think?"

Mac flung a towel onto his shoulder. "Oh yeah, sure. We'll be invadin' France in no time, and then we'll really have them krauts on the run."

Billy nodded. "You know, Mac," he said, staring at his soda, "you know how we sent all the Japanese away?"

"Sure."

"We've got a lot of full-blooded Germans living here. I think they should be sent away, too. We need to be worried about them."

Mac picked up a spoon and wiped it. "Gee, Billy. We can't send everyone away."

"I suppose." He took the last sip of his soda, echoing the shrill sound of the seltzer bottle. He leaned back and pulled a dime from his pants pocket. "Well, I better get going. I think I'm late for dinner. I'm sure my mom's waiting for me. So long, Mac."

"So long, Billy. Come back and see me real soon, my friend. And don't forget to keep yourself outta trouble."

Margaret Roarke and her son lived in a small Spanish-style home on a street lined with leafy sycamore trees. A red cement walkway flowed in a gentle curve from the sidewalk, divided the sloping lawn in two, and led to the arched front door. To the left of the door a dark green hedge grew just below the parlor window. Two red-leafed vines climbed the sides and top of the window, grazing the curved red tiles of the roof. The facade of the house seemed a frame for what hung in the middle of the window: a white flag bordered in red with a blue star sewn in its center. The blue star signified that someone in the household served in the armed forces, helping to win the war.

Mrs. Roarke stood at the sink rinsing lettuce when Billy entered the kitchen.

"Hi, Mom."

"Where have you been?" she asked without turning around.

"The radio said the Allies were moving fast past Naples, so I had to run down and get a paper."

"And?"

"And then I got a chocolate soda."

"A chocolate soda. Fine," his mother said, mildly annoyed. "Well, I still expect you to clean your plate tonight."

"Yes, Mom. I will. What are we having?"

"Lima bean casserole."

"Have we had that before?"

"No, dear. Now get ready for dinner. We're eating in five minutes."

Billy walked down the hall to his bedroom, which had recently made the transition from cowboys to sports. College pennants replaced the Western pictures on the walls. A clean, white baseball sat on his dresser, while ball caps and sports

5

equipment lay on the floor. He tossed the newspaper on his bed, then left to wash up for dinner.

Billy entered the dining room as his mother carried a casserole dish to the table. "I can't wait for the Allies to invade France, Mom. We're gonna lick the Germans for sure."

His mother didn't respond. She set the dinner down and became motionless for a moment, as if the heavy dish had anchored her arms to the table. She wiped her brow with her forearm and asked, "Have you washed for supper?"

"Yes."

"Would you say the grace tonight, please?"

They sat down and Billy bowed his head, clapped his hands together and prayed. "Dear God, bless this food and make us grateful for what we have. Bless my mother for cooking it and for working hard at the parachute factory. Please watch over my father and keep him safe. And please help him kill a lot of Germans. Amen."

Mother and son sat through supper without talking much. When they finished, Billy helped clear the table and wash the dishes. As he dried a pan, his mother asked him, "How was school today?"

"Fine."

"Did you mind Mrs. Pearson?"

"Yes, Mom. I was good today."

"Do you have homework?"

"No. I finished it right when I got home."

"Well then, when we're done I want you to brush your teeth, put your pajamas on and go straight to bed."

"Can I read in bed tonight?"

"No. I want you to go straight to sleep."

When Billy was prepared for sleep, his mother entered his room, sat on the edge of his bed and gently lifted a lock of light brown hair from his forehead. She studied his face as he lay on his back, staring back at her. His brown eyes looked as they always had, but the rest of his face was growing older. His freckles were fading and his cheeks were deflating. His nose and chin had become sharper, his eyebrows darker. His mother thought he was beautiful.

"Sweetheart, I want to talk to you about your prayer tonight."

Billy sat up on his elbows. "Yes, Mom?"

"The part about asking the Lord to kill Germans. Billy, we are not to ask God to kill people. It's fine to ask Him to keep your father safe, but it's not right to ask for people to die."

"But, Mom, we're at war with them."

"I know, darling. But those German soldiers have mothers and fathers just like you do."

"But Dad's in England, so one day he's going to fight Germans. A lot of people hate the Japanese, but I don't. They're not going to hurt Dad, but the Germans want to. They want to kill him. I can't like anyone who wants to kill my father."

His mother put a hand on his shoulder. "Listen, sweetheart, I know this is hard for you to understand, but those German soldiers would not want to hurt your father if it was not for that wicked man who rules their country."

"But . . ."

His mother interrupted him with a tender voice. "Listen, sweetheart. Just pray that God keeps Dad safe and that he comes back to us real soon. That's all you need to do."

"Well . . . can I pray that God will kill Hitler?"

His mother paused and considered.

"Yes," she said, "but not at the dinner table."

7

CHAPTER

Two

The next morning, Billy awoke alone. His mother had just left to take the Red Line streetcar to her job in downtown Los Angeles, ten miles away.

He silenced the alarm clock and walked sleepily to the bathroom down the hall to splash his face and use the toilet.

Still in his pajamas, he walked barefoot outside, onto the cold and crunchy front lawn, and claimed the morning newspaper. He read the front-page headlines as he reentered the house, then began to prepare his breakfast.

He hopped onto the counter and reached into the cupboard for a box of corn flakes, then opened the refrigerator for a bottle of milk. After pouring the flakes into a bowl, he held the bottle steady with tight hands, tilted it, and watched the milk waterfall into the cereal until it rose to the cusp of the bowl. There was no sugar in the house, so he sweetened his breakfast with honey.

While he ate, he read. During the time it took him to eat two bowls of cereal – the second sweetened with canned

8

peaches – Billy read four articles on the war before turning to the sports page.

After breakfast he brushed his teeth, dressed for school, made and packed a peanut butter and honey sandwich, and washed his dishes. He left the house, lights off and locked, to begin the long march to Woodrow Wilson Junior High School.

One block down the street, he joined Randall and their friend Charlie Saroyan, as he did every school morning.

"I'm still worried, Randall," Charlie said. "Oh, hey, Billy."

"Quit your worryin'."

"What's the matter?" Billy asked.

"Charlie here's still worried the class is gonna spill the beans about us puttin' glue on Miss Reebe's chair the day she substituted us."

"I just don't want any swats."

"Relax. No one's gonna snitch. I told Trudy if she double-crossed us, I'd kidnap that lousy mutt o' hers and mail it to Hitler's house."

"She believed that?"

"I told her I knew his address. I said, 'Hey, Trudy, his address is 195 Main St., Berlin, Germany.' She looked scared, so, yeah, she believed me."

"Did you tell everyone you were going to kidnap their dog?"

"Do I look stupid to you, Charlie? I took care of each person my own way, and I got real specific with the big mouths."

"Did you tell Spencer?" Billy asked.

"Yeah, I told goodie-goodie Spencer. I said, 'Hey, Spencer boy, you tell on us, you lousy little sissy, and I'll come over to your house and break your dolls.'"

"What'd he say?"

9

"Nothin'. He ran away. He's scared. They're all scared. We're home free, fellas."

The three boys entered the double door entrance of the two-story school building. They entered a stream of students, which seemed to carry them without effort down the hall and up the stairs to room 203, the meeting place for their seventh grade class and their beloved teacher, Mrs. Charlotte Pearson.

Their classroom was brown, black and white. Brown floor, brown shelves, brown desks, brown chairs. Black chalkboard. White walls, white ceiling. The single blast of color in the room came from the large American flag that hung near the upper right corner of the chalkboard near a framed picture of President Franklin Delano Roosevelt.

But the room was beautiful. Large windows in the wall facing the front of the school provided a magnificent mural of sky, trees and clouds for the children and their teacher. This masterpiece could be, at times, distracting, but more often proved calming and helpful to the process of thinking and learning.

On this morning the boys sat on a shelf below the windows and talked before the school bell rang. Thomas Mueller joined them.

"Hi, fellas," Thomas said. "Did you hear the *Jack Benny Show* on the radio last night? It was funny."

"It was stupid," Randall replied without interest.

"I wanted to hear it, Thomas, but my mom made me go to bed early last night," Charlie said, wanting to cool the burn of Randall's tongue.

"It was funny," Thomas repeated.

"Hey, Thomas," Randall said, "tell me again why your old man don't fight in the war."

Billy straightened his back, as if to better hear the boy's answer.

Thomas's face turned pink. "Well, I told you. He's 4-F."

"4-F? What's that? Does that mean he's a kraut or somethin'?"

"No. We are German, but we're Americans first. We don't like Hitler." The shake in his voice began to grow. "And besides, a lot of fathers aren't in the war. My pop's not the only one."

"Yeah, I know," Randall said, "but Johnny Temple's dad is about a hundred years old, so he can't go. Earl's old man is some genius who makes bombs to kill krauts. But your old man is some lousy salesman. How come he ain't in the war?"

Billy stood. "Lay off him, Randall."

Billy's response surprised him. He agreed with Randall that Germans were dangerous, that they should be sent away. He did think Thomas's situation was suspicious. And yet something inside him instinctively burst forth in defense of this boy. This German boy. Billy felt ashamed.

"No," Randall said, "I'm not going to *lay off* him. I wanna know how come our dads have to fight japs and krauts, and his old man gets to stay home and sell whatever the heck he sells."

"Furniture," Thomas said.

"What?"

"My father sells furniture."

"You gotta be foolin me. He don't even sell machine guns or somethin'? Thomas, this is ridiculous. If I was F.D.R. I'd send your whole family packin' like they did to that Fujimora jap kid. How can your old man sell furniture when we're tryin' to lick the krauts and japs in the war?"

"My father's 4-F. I told you."

"What the heck is 4-F? What the . . ."

Mrs. Pearson interrupted Randall as she entered the classroom and stood behind her desk. "Good morning, class. Please rise for the Pledge of Allegiance and our morning song."

Mrs. Pearson's arrival saved Thomas from further interrogation. For the moment.

CHAPTER

Three

Billy woke Saturday morning and grabbed the *Pasadena Star-News* from the front lawn as if it were treasure. He ran into the kitchen and startled his mother as she sat and drank a cup of coffee before work.

"Mom! It's here! Look, it's Dad!"

Billy spread the paper open to the page which featured local news. Under the heading "News of Men in Service," was an article about his father. He read it aloud.

"Promotion of Second Lieutenant William C. Roarke, of 151 S. Bonnie, Pasadena, to First Lieutenant, has been announced from the headquarters of the 101st Airborne Division, with which he is serving in Aldbourne, England. Born in Portland, Oregon, 33 years ago, Lt. Roarke has resided in Pasadena since 1924, where he attended Muir Tech High School. He graduated, with honors in engineering, from the University of Southern California in 1932, where he played baseball for three years. Lt. Roarke was married in 1930 to the former Margaret Anderson of Alhambra. They have a son, William, age 12."

"Boy, that's swell, Mom. An article on Dad. And you and I are in it."

His mother hugged him. "Yes, dear, it is wonderful, isn't it? We'll make sure we get extra copies from our neighbors. We'll send one to Grammy and Grandpa, too."

"Mom, I really miss Dad. I wish I was old enough to join up so I could help end the war and Dad could come home."

Mrs. Roarke stood and placed her cup in the sink. "Well, I'm glad you're not old enough."

"Do you have to leave for work now, Mom? Can't you stay home a little longer today?"

"No, sweetheart. I can't be late."

"Can I go to work with you today? I haven't gone with you for a long time."

"All right, but you must hurry. I'm leaving very soon."

Billy and his mother rode the Red Line to downtown Los Angeles, then walked two blocks to the parachute factory, a large new building surrounded by a near full parking lot.

"All right, dear," Mrs. Roarke said, "you know what you can do. You can have breakfast and walk around downtown, but don't go too far away, and don't walk near skid row. And make sure you spend some time at the library."

"Yes, Mom."

"Meet me at the main entrance at 12:00 sharp. I want to check on you at lunchtime."

Billy kissed his mother, then tucked the newspaper under his arm and began walking toward the heart of downtown.

The morning was hot. Not just hot for October, but hot for any month. It was as if summer had failed to use one of its days and was now given another chance to fulfill its obligations to the year.

Billy had breakfast at The Pantry, his favorite restaurant. He sat at the counter and read the newspaper while enjoying waffles and milk.

He walked to the library and picked out several books: *Spartans – Warriors of Ancient Greece, Young Teddy Roosevelt,* and *A Boy's History of Baseball.* He carried them all to the reading room, because he thought it was magnificent. He liked to pretend that this room, with its high ceiling, dark wood and elegant lamps, was the private library of his very own mansion.

He glanced through all the books, reading sections and looking at pictures. He didn't borrow any of the books, because he didn't know when he would again accompany his mother to work.

Time went by fast and Billy now had to leave and meet his mother. He returned all the books to their proper places, even though he was sure he would return in a short time to read them again.

He stepped outside and reentered the constant motion and commotion of the big city's downtown. He stood on the corner and squinted his eyes, then lifted the newspaper to shield the bright mid-day sun.

He walked the several blocks to the factory and reported to a guard stationed in a kiosk at the parking lot entrance.

"Excuse me," Billy said as he wiped sweat from his brow with his shirt sleeve, "I'm supposed to meet my mother at the main entrance there. Can I go in?"

"Okay, fella," the guard said. "Wait. Hold it a minute." Billy stopped and turned back. The guard stepped out of the kiosk and walked up to him. "How can I be sure you're not a foreign spy?"

Billy smiled. "Oh, I can assure you, sir, I'm not a spy."

"Can you now? Do you have any identification?"

"Well . . . if I were a spy I'd probably have phony identification, like an American driver's license. And I don't have *any* identification. So, I'm probably not a spy."

The guard laughed and patted Billy's shoulder. "Good enough for me, fella. You're a smart one. I hope you're on our side. You may pass."

He met his mother at the main entrance. "Billy, you're late," she said. "I've been waiting ten minutes. I started to worry about you."

"I'm sorry, Mom. I got carried away at the library."

"Did you eat? What are you going to do this afternoon? You have to meet me here at 4:00 sharp."

"I'm going back to the library, and then I'll probably go to the park. Maybe I can find some boys to play with."

"All right, dear. Please be careful. Come give me a kiss."

He kissed his mother, then traveled through a maze of cars back toward the library. As he walked between two closely parked cars, he thought he heard a strange sound. He stopped and listened closely. It sounded like crying. He turned and looked through the back seat window of an old green Ford. There he saw, lying on his back, a baby – red and sweating.

Billy stared at the baby. He thought something was wrong with the child and he wanted to help. He looked around. There was no one nearby. He didn't know what to do.

CHAPTER

Four

B illy tried to open the backseat door. The handle was hot and he quickly let go of it. He braced himself and again tried to open the door. It was locked. He tried all four doors, not caring if anyone watched him. They were all locked.

He ran to the guard. "Hey, sir," he said, panting from the run, "there's a baby locked in a car. It's hot and he's crying. He needs help."

"Hey now, slow down."

"But he doesn't look good."

"Say, aren't you the foreign spy?"

"Sorry, mister, but this isn't a joke. I'm scared about the baby."

"Look, fella, there are lots of babies in these cars, and they turn out fine. The mothers roll down the windows when it gets hot . . ."

"The windows are up. Please help."

"Where's the car?"

Billy pointed. "Over there."

"All right. Go to the car and wait for me while I get some-one to cover my duty. I'll see what I can do."

Billy ran to the car and looked in the back seat. The baby was different. His skin was white and dry. His eyes were closed and he wasn't crying. The baby lay there quiet and still.

Billy's heart jumped. The child's stillness and paleness scared him. He looked for the guard, but he wasn't coming. Billy didn't care about anything at that moment except get-ting the baby out of that car. The only way, he thought, was to break a window. How was he going to do that?

He walked swiftly through the parking lot looking for a heavy object. He couldn't find anything. The parking lot was clean.

Then he noticed a flatbed truck and ran to it, hoping it would have some tools in the back. There were no tools, but there were some copper pipes. Billy reached in the back, grabbed an L-shaped pipe and ran back to the car.

The baby was as before – pale, dry and quiet.

Billy held the pipe in his hand and stared at a front door window. He had to break it, but he didn't want glass to shower into the back seat. He tapped the window. Nothing broke. He tapped it again, harder this time, but again noth-ing cracked.

Billy now began to worry for himself. Would he get in trou-ble for breaking someone's window? Would he go to jail? He looked around and saw no one. He looked again at the baby. He knew it was hot in that car. He knew the child was in trou-ble. And he knew he had to break that window.

With two hands now on the pipe, he closed his eyes and struck a strong blow. A spider web of cracks appeared on the window. Billy started chipping away at the small broken pieces until the opening was large enough for him to put his arm through and unlock the door. He entered the car and felt a wave of heat hit him. He reached behind the seat to unlock the back door, then went out to open it.

He carefully lifted the child and carried it outside, holding it to his chest. He felt the baby breathing, but was surprised that he was quiet. The crash of the window and the lifting by a stranger did not make the baby cry. Billy wanted him to cry, to reassure him that he was all right.

"Hey, little baby," he said softly, "are you okay?" He rubbed the top of the child's head. "Hey, little fella, cry. It's all right; you can cry now."

Billy carefully carried the child to the kiosk.

"Woah! How'd you get that baby?" the guard said.

"I broke a window. He needs help. He's not crying. Please call a doctor."

The guard dialed the factory and asked them to send the plant's doctor right away to Entrance 1.

"I'm sorry I couldn't come and help you, son," the guard said. "I asked for someone to cover me, but no one came. If I left my post, it would mean my job."

"Do you think he'll be all right?"

The guard looked closely at the baby's face. "You were right, son. He doesn't look good."

The doctor arrived and set his open black bag on the ground. Without a word, he took the child from Billy's arms and shook it gently. The baby gave a weak cry and moved its arms. The doctor put his ear to the child's face and felt its breath, then shone a light into its eyes, which were now half-open.

"Is he going to be all right?" Billy asked.

The doctor didn't answer. He handed the baby to the guard, then wrapped a cuff on the infant's arm and checked his blood pressure. He put a finger on his neck and felt his pulse, then took his temperature.

After reading the thermometer, the doctor looked up at the guard. "Who got the baby out of the car?"

"The boy did, Doc."

The doctor turned to Billy. "You did the right thing. This baby could have been in serious danger."

"Is he going to be all right?"

"He needs fluids. I'll take him to my office and watch him awhile, but I think he's going to be fine."

As the doctor carried the child away, the guard put a hand on Billy's shoulder. "What's your name, fella?"

"Billy. Billy Roarke."

"You're a hero, Billy Roarke," he said. "A real hero."

Someone finally came to relieve him, so the guard walked with Billy to the factory and led him to an unoccupied office with large windows that looked onto the factory floor.

"Now wait here," he said. "I'll be back."

Billy sat in a chair and looked at the machinery – its parts moving at great speeds, producing great sounds. The workers stood beside the machines, each with tasks that were repeated like the rhythm of breathing – regular and steady, without the hindrance of thought.

After some time he saw the guard following a pretty young woman in a smart-looking skirt and jacket. She opened the door and flashed a big smile. The woman had brilliant blonde hair and bright red lipstick that framed her white teeth like a sliced radish. She spoke rapidly, as if she were late for a date.

"Is this the little boy who saved my baby?" she asked the guard without looking at him.

"This is him, Miss. Billy Roarke's his name," the guard said proudly.

Billy stood to shake her hand. "I'm glad I could help you, ma'am."

"Oh and aren't you sweet, too. I just don't know how I'm gonna thank you."

"You don't need to . . ."

"Now I know that my baby was just fine in that car, but you did a brave thing breakin' my window to save him."

"Uh, Miss," the guard said, "the baby was looking . . ."

The woman ignored the guard and continued speaking to Billy. "Oh I'm sure you thought you were doin' a good thing, but I've had my baby in my car since I've been workin' here and I've had no problems. A lot of the girls do that, you know. My husband's in the Navy and my folks are back home so I've got nowhere else."

"Gee," Billy said, "I just thought . . ."

"And now I don't know *what* I am goin' to do, because now I've got a broken window and how am I gonna put my baby in a car with a broken window?"

"I'm sorry, ma'am."

"Well now I know you are and I'm not blamin' you. You're just a sweet little boy who didn't know what he was doin'. Your mama brought you to work 'cause she didn't know what to do with you, just like I had to bring my baby to work. Now isn't that right?"

"Well . . ."

"Now what's your mama's name, honey?"

"Margaret Roarke, ma'am."

"Margaret Roarke," the woman said as she bent over a desk to write on a piece of paper. "Now isn't that a pretty name?"

"Yes, ma' . . ."

"I wouldn't know your mama, honey, on account of I'm a secretary. But you give your mama this piece of paper. It has my name and department, and she can pay me for my window. I couldn't expect a sweet little boy like you to be able to pay for my window. I think ten dollars would be good."

"Now, look here, Miss," the guard said, "this boy . . ."

"Oh now, I know he meant well, but now I've got a problem and I'm goin' to see to it that it's fixed."

The woman gave the paper to Billy and pinched his cheek. "You're a cute little boy. Now make sure your mama pays me. I'd like the money on Monday."

"Yes, ma'am."

"I think you've done a terrible thing, Miss," the guard said as she walked to the door.

The woman stopped and looked at the guard. "Did you ever have to bring your baby to work, Mista?"

"No, Miss, but I . . ."

"I didn't think so."

Billy was now afraid of his mother's reaction to the incident. He waited impatiently for the horn to blow the end of her shift.

Mrs. Roarke was told everything before she met Billy in the office. She said nothing as she approached him; he remained seated, unsure of what to say to her. She bent down, hugged him tightly and gave him a big kiss. When she stepped back, he saw that his mother had been crying.

"You're not mad at me?"

"Mad?" Mrs. Roarke put a hand on her chest as if to suppress more crying. "Oh, Billy, I'm so proud of you."

"What about the ten dollars?"

"I paid the ten dollars, sweetheart. I don't care about the ten dollars."

"Can we go home now?"

She smiled. "Since we're downtown I thought I'd treat you. We can go to dinner wherever you'd like."

"That's swell, Mom. How about going to the Mexican neighborhood, Olvera Street. I pick that."

"Olvera Street it is. Oh, Billy. As soon as we get home I am going to write your father and tell him what a wonderful deed you have done. He will be *so* proud of you."

A warmth he had never felt before moved through Billy and gave him the biggest smile of his life.

CHAPTER

Five

Billy bought a Christmas present for his father on Olvera Street, a pair of handmade leather gloves. He needed to mail it in October so his father would receive it in December.

The next Saturday morning, with Mrs. Roarke at work, Billy went into his mother's bedroom and opened her top dresser drawer. He looked for paper and twine to wrap the gift, but instead found an unfinished letter his mother was writing to his father. He lifted it from the drawer and read it.

> *"My Darling,*
> *I know I shouldn't have but I found the*
> *smartest pair of shoes. Please forgive me.*
> *They weren't cheap, but you will look so*
> *handsome in them. They wait here for you.*
> *I realize in my last letter I went on and on*
> *about Billy saving the baby, but I was so*
> *proud. I know you would be, too. He is so*

*like you, darling. Sometimes that helps me
and sometimes it makes everything so much
worse . . ."*

Billy returned the letter, wondering what it was about him that made things "so much worse" for his mother. He found the paper and twine and wrapped his father's gift, then walked several blocks to the post office and mailed the package.

When he returned home he waited for Charlie and Randall, who arrived shortly with their wooden wagons, ready to help win the war.

The "Tin Can Commandoes" ventured about a mile beyond their neighborhood this day to collect donations for the war effort. They would carry the metal and rubber items in their wagons, then roll the cargo to the collection site at their school. As they walked, they chanted rhymes and sang songs.

> *"Whistle while you work,*
> *Hitler is a jerk,*
> *Mussolini is a weeny,*
> *And Tojo wears a skirt."*

The first house they came to was a pretty white bungalow with a porch covered in potted flowers. An elderly woman opened the door.

"Yes?" she said. "Hello, gentlemen. What can I do for you?"

"Good morning, ma'am," Billy said. "We're the 'Tin Can Commandoes,' and we're collecting metal and rubber for the war. Do you have anything you'd like to donate?"

25

"Oh, aren't you marvelous. How gallant of you to be spending your Saturday working to help our boys overseas. Please give me a moment and I'll check." The woman returned with an old metal cake pan. "I'm afraid I've already given so many of my things away, but I do hope you can use this."

"Yes, ma'am," Billy said as he took the pan from the woman. "This is great. Thank you."

The house next door displayed a service flag in the front window. But this flag was different than the one that hung in Billy's house. This one had a gold star sewn in its field of white. A gold star which meant that the member of this household who served in the armed forces had been killed.

Billy stopped and stared at the star. He thought about the blue star on his service flag and how he could never imagine it becoming a gold one. As much as Billy worried about his father, he could never truly believe that he would be killed in the war. He would come home again. Maybe wounded, maybe hurt, but alive. Alive and well enough to play ball with him again. Well enough to take him to the mountains and teach him about the trees and the birds, the rivers and the lakes, and the life they held within them. Well enough to read to him at bedtime. The stories of knights and dragons, of heroes and the evil they destroy. His father would come back and do all the things he did before. All of them. His father would not die.

Randall interrupted his thoughts. "C'mon, what are ya waiting for, Billy? Let's go."

"No," he said. "Let's skip this house."

Later that morning, the trio knocked on a door that was answered by a young girl in a puffy blue dress. She looked to be in about the fifth grade and appeared suspicious of the boys.

"Hello," she said.

"Uh," Billy said, "is your mother home?"

"No. No one's home but me, so I have to go now." She started to shut the door.

"Hey, girl," Randall said, "we're just here to collect junk for the war. Ya got any junk?"

"See here, you *mean* boy. I'm not allowed to talk to strange boys, and you are . . ."

"Hey, you look here, Little Miss Muffet . . ."

"Randall, stop. I'm sorry, girl, if we scared you," Billy said in a calm and friendly manner. "We're just going around collecting metal and rubber for the war. If you have something to donate, that would be great."

"Okay. I know where some metal is," she said cheerfully before skipping away.

The girl returned with a polished wooden box. "Here," she said as she handed it to Billy. "There's metal in there."

He opened the box. Shiny bracelets, jewels and rings reflected light in every direction, creating a kaleidoscope of brightness and color that was almost blinding.

"Wow!" the boys said together.

"Gee, do you think your mother would want to give this away?" Billy asked. "This looks like something she would want to keep."

"She never wears any of those things. She hasn't worn them in a long time, so I don't think she likes them. You can have them."

"Say, those would make some swell bullets," Charlie said.

"Don't be a dope," Randall said. "They wouldn't use them things to make bullets. They use stuff like that for bombs."

Billy gently placed the jewelry case in his wagon.

"Wait," the girl said. "I better take the box. My mother *loves* that. She polishes it all the time."

"Oh sure," Billy said. He carefully spilled the jewelry into the cake pan, creating a thousand tinkling sounds all at once. "Here ya go."

"Thank you," the girl said as she reclaimed the case. "Okay bye."

The boys said goodbye as they pulled their wagons to the next house, the jewels jangling in the rusted tin pan.

An hour later they found their wagons full of donated items and decided to try one more house before delivering the goods. A woman answered the door of a small house with a neatly tended lawn and garden.

"Thank God you're here," she said after their introduction. "My husband collects everything. Nothing but dirty old junk. Never throws a lick of it away. You wait here quiet-like. He's in the back, working in the garden."

The woman returned with a tin cigar box filled with keys, a few golf balls, a souvenir coin from the Chicago World's Fair, along with a bronze trophy with the engraving:

Curly Ed Gilroy
Moose of the Year, 1933
Loyal Order of Moose, Lodge 706
Waukegan, Illinois

"Here, take this junk," she said. "My home feels cleaner already."

The boys balanced the items on the towering piles, not taking the time to read the trophy's inscription. They thanked the woman and headed for school, carefully pulling their loaded wagons.

One block later, as they were about to turn onto Colorado Boulevard, Charlie noticed a man running toward them holding a long object.

"My Moose trophy!" he shouted as he ran, holding a pair of hedge trimmers. "Hey, gimme back my Moose trophy!"

"Hey, fellas," Charlie said, "look! Some guy's coming after us, yelling something."

"What's he saying?" Billy asked, who along with Randall and Charlie now stopped to observe the man.

"My Moose trophy!" the man continued to shout. "My Moose trophy! Hey, gimme . . ."

"Holy Toledo!" Randall cried. "He's a wop spy. He's yellin' somethin' about Mussolini. And he's got a sword! Run for it!"

The boys didn't wait for confirmation of Randall's theory. They ran down busy Colorado, pulling their wagons, which now spilled keys and pans and cans and rings, shouting, "Gangway, help! An Italian spy is trying to kill us! Help, help! Gangway!"

Several men stopped to look for someone chasing the boys and saw no one. "Crazy kids," one said.

They dragged their wagons one more block to Himmelfarb's and noisily entered the drug store, clanging their wagons against the door frame.

"Woah. What's goin' on, fellas?" Mac asked from behind the counter.

"Mac, an Italian spy is chasing us down the street!" Billy said.

"No, kiddin'," Mac replied in disbelief. "Italian spy, huh?"

"Yeah," Charlie said. "We think we're in the clear now. We lost him in the crowd. He must've wanted all the stuff we collected for the war."

"No foolin'," Randall said. "We got ourselves some swell bomb-makin' stuff." He reached into Billy's wagon to scoop a handful of the jewelry from the cake pan, most of which survived the bumpy ride. "Get a load o' this stuff."

"Wow! Say, who gave you fellas that?"

"A girl," Billy said. "Her mother didn't want it."

A few minutes later the clanging of bells caused the boys to quickly turn their heads toward the door. A man entered and sat at the counter. "Coffee, Mac," he said.

"Comin' right up."

"Hiya, boys," the man said to the trio, who were greatly relieved he was not the one chasing them with a sword. "Hey, Mackey, Pasadena's finest just caught themselves a big fish. A real whopper."

"Ya don't say," Mac replied as he poured the man a cup of coffee.

"Yessir. Just down the street. Saw it myself." The man squinted and took a measured sip of the hot black coffee, then set the mug on the counter. "Italian spy."

Mac's face turned to the boys, whose eyes widened and mouths opened.

"No kidding, mister?" Billy said. "The police caught him? He was chasing *us*. He wanted our stuff for the war."

"Oh sure, kid. I'm sure he wanted your . . ."

Randall showed the man a handful of the jewels.

"Uh . . . oh . . . I see," the man said. "Well, you can relax now, boys. I saw the police escorting the guy into a squad car myself. He kept yellin' somethin' about Mussolini."

"Yep, that's him," Billy said.

"Boy, I'll tell ya," Mac said, "it's a sad day in America when the streets of Pasadena aren't safe for young fellas like this. Step up to the counter, boys. The sodas are on the house."

After Billy came home and explained the entire episode to his mother, Mrs. Roarke called the Pasadena Police Department and was told that no Italian spies had been arrested that day. The next morning she carefully searched the *Pasadena Star-News* and found no mention of Italian spies. That night Billy went to bed without his dinner.

CHAPTER

Six

One can't tell it's Christmas time in Pasadena by the weather. Snow doesn't cover the ground, only the peaks of the nearby San Gabriel Mountains. The air is crisp, not frozen. But the town, nonetheless, reveals the season. Decorations adorn storefront windows and Santa Claus is in the department store.

On Christmas Eve evening Mrs. Roarke brought cookies and eggnog to the parlor. She turned the radio on low to a station that was playing Handel's *Messiah*, and together mother and son finished reading *A Christmas Carol* by Charles Dickens.

Every year since Billy was three years old, the Roarkes would gather near the fireplace and take turns reading aloud from the short novel. Billy started reading from the book when he was five, and in only two more years he required no help with the words. They started about a week before Christmas, making sure they would finish on Christmas Eve. Tonight they were to read "Stave Five," the last section entitled "The End of It."

They each read a page at a time. Billy tried an English accent when reading, as his father used to, while his mother kept her voice.

When they finished, Billy and his mother congratulated each other on completing the book yet again. Billy said that he had read in the paper that this year was the one hundredth anniversary of the book, and that he hoped his great-great grandchildren would be reading it one hundred years from now.

He ate more cookies while his mother poked the fire. She turned off the lamp, and together they watched the flames and listened to the radio.

Billy studied the Christmas tree, bare of lights and in need of new ornaments. He didn't mind that. What he missed this Christmas had nothing to do with tinsel and lights. What he wanted most was to hear three voices reading *A Christmas Carol*. He looked at his mother and knew that she wanted the same thing.

On Christmas morning Billy and his mother sat by the tree and opened presents. "I'm going to open Dad's first," he said. The boy grabbed the large brown envelope and ripped it open. From it he pulled a homemade book made of heavy sketching paper bound with string. On the cover was the neatly printed title: "The Adventures of Billy Roarke."

"Wow! Dad made a book about me. Look, Mom."

"That's beautiful, dear."

The cover illustration showed Billy sitting on a horse dressed in a cowboy suit, complete with a ten-gallon hat and a sheriff's badge. He flipped the pages and saw himself in all sorts of scenes. In one chapter he was a Brooklyn Dodger winning the World Series; in another a Southern Cal football player scoring a touchdown in the Rose Bowl. One episode found him as a pilot shooting down German war planes. Each page was illustrated in colored pencil and each story written in perfect handwriting that rested on straight, lightly-penciled lines. Billy read the entire book to his mother before opening any other presents.

"That's the best present I've ever had. I'll keep that forever."

"It's *very* special, sweetheart. It's a wonderful gift."

"Okay, Mom, now you open your present from Dad."

Mrs. Roarke opened a small package that held a thin gold bracelet. She clasped it around her wrist, then stared at it as she softly stroked it with her finger.

"Okay," Billy said as his mother looked up, "now I'll open my present from Grammy and Grandpa." He tore the brown paper wrapping and revealed a model airplane kit. "Wow! A B-24 Liberator bomber. That's swell. Gee, I wish they could be here this Christmas."

"I do, too. Grandpa tried hard to save his gasoline stamps, but it's just too far from Oregon."

"I read that some people cheat with their stamps."

"Your grandfather doesn't cheat. He didn't raise your father to cheat, and we didn't raise you that way, either. Now, open your gift from me."

His mother's gift to him was a complete football uniform: jersey, pants and leather helmet.

"Gee, thanks, Mom. This is great. And it's red, too. Like U.S.C."

"I'm glad you like it. The helmet is used, but the rest of the uniform is brand new."

"It's swell. Thank you. Can I wear it today?"

"You can wear it for a while, but not at dinner. We're having guests, remember?"

Billy jumped up. "When are they coming? I can't wait."

"They'll be here at 2:00. I want you to wear your red tie and blue jacket. You look very smart in that outfit."

"Ah, Mom, do I have to?"

"Yes, you have to. Now, there seems to be one gift left."

Billy sat down again. "That's for you. From me."

"My goodness."

Billy gave his mother a photograph of himself that he had pasted to a piece of wood. On the edges of the wood he had nailed flattened bottle caps to create a shiny metallic frame.

"This is beautiful."

"Thanks. Maybe I should have donated the bottle caps for the war, but . . ."

"Oooh," Mrs. Roarke said suddenly.

"What's the matter?"

"I seemed to have cut myself on the frame."

He came closer to his mother. "Oh, I'm sorry. Mom, you're bleeding. I'm sorry. I should have known those bottle caps would be too sharp. It's all my fault."

Mrs. Roarke stayed seated and held her bleeding finger. "It's not your fault, sweetheart. It's a beautiful gift. I should have been more careful."

Billy hugged his mother and pressed his cheek into hers. "I'm sorry I hurt you, Mom. I'll never hurt you again. I promise."

Mrs. Roarke let go of her finger and hugged him back. "I know you won't, sweetheart," she said. "I know you won't."

CHAPTER

Seven

The doorbell rang and Billy ran to it. "They're here, Mom! They're here!"

"Slow down, sweetheart. We don't want to scare them."

He opened the door and saw two tall and smiling young men in uniform, one holding a box of candy, the other a bouquet of flowers.

The one with the candy bent down and said to Billy, "Maybe you can help us, fella. We're looking for the Roarke house. We understand they serve up a swell Christmas dinner and we'd like to get in on it."

"This is the Roarke house." Billy smiled. "You're supposed to be here."

"Well, how about that. I thought this house smelled awful good. Put 'er there, young Roarke."

"Yes, sir," he said as he shook the man's hand.

"My name's Sam, and this here's my good pal Andy."

"How are you, son?" Andy said.

"Good. And this is my mom."

Mrs. Roarke came to the door. "Please come in, gentlemen," she said.

Both men removed their hats. "Thank you, ma'am," Sam said. "We're much obliged, Mrs. Roarke, for having us to Christmas dinner. Andy and I brought you some candy." Sam handed her the box, then turned to Billy. "And for you, young fella, we got you some flowers." Sam took the bouquet from Andy and gave it to the boy. "You like flowers, don't you?"

"Uh, yes, sir."

"Ah, don't call me sir; I'm just a private. Call me Sam. And put those in some water, will ya?"

"Maybe he can call you Private Sam," Mrs. Roarke said, thinking about her son's manners. "Please have a seat. What can I get the two of you to drink while I finish dinner?"

"Ma'am," Sam said, "after what they give us at camp, cod liver oil would taste great. Whatever you've got."

"Well, we have egg nog, tea, orange pop and some . . ."

"Sign me up for orange pop," Sam said. "Andy, the same?"

"Sure."

Sam and Andy sat on the sofa while Mrs. Roarke took the flowers from Billy and returned to the kitchen.

"So, what's your name, fella?" Sam asked.

"Billy."

"Billy, huh? Well that's a fine name, but it needs something more. You ever been in the Marines?"

"No, sir."

"Well in that sharp outfit you've got on there, you look like you outrank us. How about we call you Sergeant Billy?"

He smiled. "That'd be swell."

As the two men sat and sipped orange pop, Billy showed them the article about his father, the Christmas book he had received, and his baseball and mitt.

After reading the article and the book, Andy said, "Your father sounds like quite a man, Billy."

"Sure does," Sam said. "A real swell guy, I'll bet."

"You fellas sure are nice. Can you spend the night?"

The two men laughed. "I'm afraid not, Sergeant Billy," Sam said. "Our sergeant wouldn't much like us being AWOL."

"That means 'Absent Without Leave,'" Billy said.

"That's right," Sam replied. "I'm afraid we've only got ourselves a day pass."

"Dinner is served, gentlemen," Mrs. Roarke said as she carried a platter holding a large roasted turkey to the dining table.

The men joined her. "Mrs. Roarke," Sam said, "this is sure some spread. How about this, Andy?"

"This is terrific, ma'am. Thank you."

Mrs. Roarke pointed to all the dishes on the table. "We have potatoes, green beans, gravy, cranberries and bread. Oh, and I'll need one of you nice gentlemen to carve the turkey."

"I got high marks in bayonet training," Sam said. "I'll give it a whirl."

Sam sliced the turkey and passed it to the plates while the others served themselves from the side dishes.

"Now then," Mrs. Roarke said, "would one of you care to say the grace?"

"I will, ma'am," Andy said. Everyone bowed their heads. "For what we are about to receive, Dear Lord, make us grateful. And bless Mrs. Roarke and her son for opening their home to us this Christmas day. Amen."

The table was quiet as everyone started eating.

After a few mouthfuls, Sam said, "Mrs. Roarke, after living on camp food I can honestly say I've never enjoyed a meal more than this one."

"Well, thank goodness turkeys aren't rationed. I got a good one this time."

"It's all very delicious, ma'am," Andy said.

"Thank you. So what is Uncle Sam's plan for you boys?"

"We ship out next week," Sam said. "And I can't wait. I really want a piece of the action." Sam pointed a knife at Billy. "And I'm gonna get me a jap for you."

"Hey, thanks."

Mrs. Roarke gave Billy a disapproving look.

"The way I see it," Sam said, "this war is like a football game. I played football in high school back home and . . ."

"You did?"

"You bet, Sergeant Billy. I was a halfback. All-league, too. Yep, I can't wait to get out there and give them japs a real lickin'." Sam took a bite of turkey and continued talking. "I think my football skills will help me in battle. I'm strong and fast, and I can't wait to get me some jap in hand-to-hand. I'm itchin' to go, brother."

"Wow," Billy said. "You're gonna kill a lot of japs!"

His mother gave him an even sterner look and said sharply, "*Billy.*"

"Sorry to get the boy riled up, Mrs. Roarke. I'm just real excited about my chance to get in there."

"That's quite all right. I understand."

"Did you play football, Private Andy?" Billy asked.

He swallowed his mouthful before answering. "Sure I did. I played baseball, too."

"Gee, I bet you can't wait to get over there."

"Well, I just want this war to end. I guess I'm just not as brave as my friend Sam here."

"Aw, you're brave. I'll bet you'll kill a lot of japs."

"*Billy!*" his mother said with a look that said shut up.

"That's okay, Mrs. Roarke," Andy said. "You see, Billy, I want to do my duty and serve my country, but I don't know what it's going to be like over there. Maybe it'll be like a football game, but I don't know. I guess I'm just kind of nervous right now." Andy dropped his head a bit and set his fork on his plate. "I'm sorry, everybody. I didn't mean to spoil your Christmas dinner."

Sam put his hand on Andy's arm. "You're fine, buddy."

Mrs. Roarke looked at Andy with damp eyes.

"Are you scared of dying, Private Andy?" Billy asked.

Andy took a sip of water, then wiped his mouth with the napkin from his lap. He looked at the boy. "Yes, Billy," he said. "I am scared of dying."

After dinner Mrs. Roarke served cookies and tea in the living room. She alertly turned all conversation away from the war. Instead, she got the young men to talk about their hometowns, families and friends. Sam told jokes, and together they listened to the radio.

The young soldiers left in the early evening. They had written down the Roarke's address, and both promised to write. Mrs. Roarke said they would remember the young men in their prayers.

Billy was sad to see them leave. He had become quite fond of both men and kept offering ways to keep them around. They finally agreed to one of his suggestions. As soon as they could, they would all once again share a Christmas day dinner.

CHAPTER
Eight

On a Sunday afternoon in late January, Billy sat alone with a banana split at the counter in Himmelfarb's. "Hey, Mac," he said, "did you hear they picked General Eisenhower to lead the invasion into France?"

"Sure did. I hear old Ike, as they call him, is a swell choice."

Billy spoke while chewing on a cherry. "Yeah. I read that, too. I can't wait. We're really gonna get them krauts."

Mac took the towel off his shoulder and started wiping the counter. "You bet we will."

"Tell me a war story, Mac. Tell me a real good one."

"Aw, you don't want to hear a war story. There's nothin' to tell."

"Sure there is. There must be. You must've had a whole bunch of adventures." He paused to fill his mouth with whipped cream. He swallowed, then said, "Was it like a football game, with fellas beating each other up? Is that what a battle is like?"

Mac's voice softened and sounded puzzled. "A football game?" He stared at the counter that he'd just stopped wiping.

"No, Billy. It's not like a football game. It's not like any kind o' game."

"So . . . it's pretty bad?"

"It's worse than anything you can think up in your head."

"Oh."

"The only good thing is knowin' that you're standin' up to the worst the devil can throw at ya."

Billy ate a few more bites before talking again. "Why did you do it then? I mean, how could you stand it?"

Mac flung the towel back on his shoulder, but kept his eyes on the counter. "Ya do it 'cause you have to. Ya do it for your pal. Ya don't leave the mud and the rats and the maggots and the noise, because ya can't leave your pal who's sharin' your hole in the mud. Ya got nothin' but time, so ya know him better'n ya know anyone else. Ya know that you want him to get home more than ya want yourself to get home. Ya know about his apple farm. Ya know about his girl. I never saw a picture of her, but I know exactly what she looks like. I know the sound of her voice, and I know how much she wanted to see him back home, cause he read me every letter she wrote a hundred times. I'll never forget one word from them letters. They got muddy and torn, and ripped and finally destroyed, but we both had them memorized. We weren't gonna let them letters die."

"Did your friend . . ."

"I know everything there is to know 'bout growin' apples. I could start my own apple farm right now. I know when to pick 'em, how much water they need, what to do when the freeze comes. Yep, I could do that all right."

"Why did you want to enlist again?"

His eyes returned to the boy. "I believe in this fight. And besides, I've already been through it. I can handle it. I figure, take me instead of some kid." Mac paused. "I just wanted to save some kid from hell."

Billy didn't sleep well that night. For the first time he became terrified for his father. He had never fully believed that anything terrible could happen to him. His father was strong. He was smart. He was always happy, gentle and kind. No harm could ever come to someone like that.

Billy lay in bed thinking about what Mac had said. How he made war sound so bad and so much worse than what he thought before. So much worse than what he saw in the movies. Heroes never died in the movies.

But Billy's hero wasn't in a movie. Or a football game. Billy's hero was in a war, and there was nothing he could do to save him. Nothing he could do to save his father from hell.

*****

Billy wasn't hungry the next morning. He lingered over a bowl of cereal until he became late for school.

He left the house, but didn't walk faster than normal, even though Charlie and Randall had already left without him.

The clouds were in a single sheet, covering the entire sky, making a field of dirty gray with no streaks of sunlight able to crack through. Mist fell and blurred the sharp outlines of the mountains and trees. The air was heavy and seemed to weigh on Billy, pushing his shoulders, head and the corners of his mouth down. He was not happy.

In class he kept his head down and did his work, not sharing his usual smiles and words with classmates.

During lunchtime he tried to sit away from his friends, but they abandoned their usual table and sat with him.

"What's doin', Billy?" Randall asked. "What's the big idea ditchin' your pals?"

"Nothin'. I'm just eating my lunch."

"No kiddin'. Look, Charlie, Billy's just eatin' his lunch. Since when do you eat here? Well, we're not too good for ya, so we'll join ya."

"Be my guest."

"Hey, what're you so sore about?"

"Nothin'. I'm not sore."

"You okay, Billy?" Charlie asked.

"Yeah, sure. I'm okay."

"Well, I'm positive now," Randall began, "that that no-good, lousy kraut next door to me is a spy."

"Go on," Charlie said.

"You go on, Charlie. You wouldn't know a Nazi spy if he bit ya on the nose. This guy's a spy, I'm tellin' ya. I got proof."

"What proof?"

"What proof? You tell me Mr. Know-it-all what some normal American citizen is doin' with German books, written in German. Huh? Explain that one."

"How do you know he has German books?"

Randall took a bite from his sandwich, but spoke anyway. "'Cause I looked in his trash, smart guy. And you tell me why he's throwin' that stuff away if it's not top secret."

"I thought your neighbor's name was Mr. La Pierre. That's not a German name."

"Don't be a dope, Charlie. Ya think a kraut spy is gonna have a kraut name? 'Hiya, neighbors, my name is Adolf Krautspy. Pleased to make your acquaintance.'"

"I don't know. You think everyone's a spy."

"Well, let's ask our own kraut what *he* thinks. Hey, Thomas, come here."

Thomas obeyed, leaving his nearby table to stand near the boys. "Yes? Hi, fellas."

"Hey, Thomas," Randall said, "you bein' a kraut, you'd be able to tell if someone was a kraut spy, right?"

"No, I don't think so."

"Hey, fellas, maybe Thomas and his old man are spies sellin' secrets in that lousy furniture he sells." Randall laughed.

"No, Randall, we're not spies."

"Well anyways, you're a kraut, and bein' a kraut you could probably tell one of your own, right?"

"I don't know; it depends on . . ."

"Why don't you just leave?" Billy said to Thomas.

"What, Billy?"

"You heard me. Just go back to your table."

"Sure, Billy, I'll leave." Thomas slowly walked away.

"What're you sore at him for, Billy?" Charlie said. "He didn't do anything."

"Why don't you guys beat it. Just go back to your table."

"Sure. We'll go back to our table. C'mon, Charlie," Randall said. "Billy don't want no company right now."

After school, Randall and Charlie waited fifteen minutes for Billy, who was talking to Mrs. Pearson in class. They joined him on the playground for the walk home, but Billy didn't talk until he spotted Thomas, who had returned to school to play.

"Hey, Thomas!" Billy shouted as he approached the boy, who was standing alone holding a big red ball. "Get out of here! Go home!"

"What?" Thomas said.

"Billy? What's wrong with you?" Charlie asked.

"You heard me, you dirty kraut! Get out of this school! Get

out of this country!" Billy now stood several yards from Thomas.

"Why don't you leave me alone, Billy? I've never done anything to you."

"Oh yeah? You're a Hitler lover!"

"No, I'm not. I told you, we don't like Hitler. Now just stop it, Billy. Just leave me alone."

"No! I won't leave you alone! Why does my dad have to go and fight, and your dad stays home? Huh, Thomas, huh?"

Billy moved closer and pushed the boy, just hard enough to force Thomas to take a step back to keep his balance. The red ball rolled away.

Thomas started to cry. "I told you, Billy. He's 4-F. They won't take him. Now please just leave me alone!"

"No! Your dad's a kraut! And a coward! He won't fight 'cause he's afraid!"

"Leave me alone!" Thomas screamed. "Go away and leave me alone!"

"No, Billy, don't!" Charlie cried.

Billy did not hear him. He heard nothing as he threw Thomas to the ground, sat on his stomach and pounded his face with his right hand. Thomas cried out for him to stop, his words broken by Billy's blows.

Charlie tried to reach Billy and tear him off Thomas, but Randall grabbed his arm and said, "Stay out of it, Charlie. It's their fight."

The carnage continued. Blood from Thomas's face and mouth splattered onto Billy with each strike. He punched now with both hands while Thomas's head bounced on the hard dirt ground.

Thomas's cries now began to decrease. He was tiring and becoming numb to the attack.

Billy, too, began to tire. He felt himself slowly return to his right mind, where he could hear, see and feel. His hands throbbed. His stomach was tight. He stopped hitting Thomas. He stopped and remained seated on his stomach, staring at what he had done. He slowly rolled off the boy and landed on his knees next to him.

Charlie was crying. Randall stood silently. Thomas was quiet and unmoving. Still on his knees, Billy bent over, put his face in his hands and wept. First quietly, and then with deep, deep groans that convulsed his body and seemed to shake the ground.

Two teachers now approached the scene. Upon viewing the wreckage, they ran quickly back to the school building, one to retrieve ice and bandages, the other to call for an ambulance.

CHAPTER

Nine

Billy's mother came home from work and saw her son sitting on the sofa, staring at nothing.   "What's happened?" she asked.

His statued look crumbled as he ran crying to her, wrapping his arms around her waist and burying his head in her belly.

"What's happened, sweetheart?"

"Oh, Mom," he cried, "I beat a boy! I beat him real bad!"

"What boy? Why? What happened?"

"I don't know! I'm sorry! I'm sorry!"

Mrs. Roarke stepped back from her son's embrace, held his shoulders firmly, bent down and looked in his eyes. "Billy," she said firmly, "tell me what happened."

"I beat up Thomas Mueller. I beat him bad. I beat him 'cause he's German and his dad's not in the war. I'm sorry, Mom; I'm sorry!"

"Oh my God, Billy. Where is he now?"

"I don't know. The ambulance took him."

"The ambulance? Oh my God!" She released her hands from his shoulders, stepped back and walked briskly to the phone. She called for a cab, sat alone, and did not say another word to her son until both were seated in the waiting room of Huntington Memorial Hospital.

"Mrs. Roarke?"

"Yes, nurse."

"The boy you inquired about, Thomas Mueller, has been released." The nurse looked at Billy. "Well, how nice of you to come visit your friend. Cheer up, young man. I'm sure you can visit him at home."

"Is he okay?"

"He'll be fine. Don't worry. Your job now is to cheer him up. Now don't be such a Gloomy Gus. How can your friend feel better when you look like that?"

"Yes, ma'am."

When they returned home, Mrs. Roarke dialed the operator and asked for the Mueller family phone number. As she hung up Billy asked her, "Do you want me to talk to them, Mom?"

"Go to your room."

Mrs. Roarke dialed the number. Mr. Mueller answered the phone. As soon as she introduced herself, he hung up.

She sat by the phone with her head resting on her hand, eyes closed. In a few moments the phone rang and she answered in mid-ring. It was the school secretary requesting that she and Billy meet with the principal tomorrow morning at 9:00. Mrs. Roarke agreed and hung up. She remained by the phone, head again on hand, eyes closed, mind wide open. She didn't sleep that night.

Billy and his mother entered the principal's office and stood in front of his desk.

Mr. Kline was a big-chested man in a nice suit. He stood, motioned for the two of them to have a seat, then seated himself without a greeting. He removed his glasses and folded his hands on his desk.

"Mrs. Roarke," he began, "I don't think I need to explain the severity of this situation."

"No, Mr. Kline, you don't."

"The beating administered to our young Thomas Mueller by your son was nothing short of criminal."

"Is he going to be okay?" Billy asked in a whisper.

"Yes, Mr. Roarke. He has survived, if that is your concern."

Billy dropped his head, stared at the dark wood grain of the desk, and said nothing.

"I would like to speak with the family, Mr. Kline," Mrs. Roarke said, "and offer them anything I can."

"I'm afraid that won't be possible. They refused to be here for this meeting and do not want to associate in any way with your boy or his family. Their wish is for their son to never again set eyes on your boy."

"Is there anything I can do for them without their knowing it?"

"No, I'm afraid not. As I said, they want nothing whatsoever to do with your family. Please drop the matter."

"Yes, Mr. Kline."

"Now to the business of your young man. As principal of this school it is my duty to assure the safety and well-being of all my students. That duty requires the removal of dangerous elements who threaten the safety of the children in my charge. Therefore, Mrs. Roarke, your son, at the moment the school board signs the papers this evening, will be officially dismissed from this school. Expelled. Never again to set foot on this campus."

Billy's eyes remained on the desk. His mouth remained closed.

Mrs. Roarke's voice shook. "Where will he go?"

"That is no longer my concern, Mrs. Roarke."

"Yes," she said in an almost silent voice, "of course."

"Are there any more questions?"

"No, Mr. Kline, no more questions," Mrs. Roarke said as she and Billy stood to leave. "Good day."

Mrs. Roarke had to work the swing shift that day because of the meeting that morning. She did not speak to Billy and did not answer him when he asked her where he would attend school. In the afternoon Charlie and Randall came to the door, but she told them Billy could not see them.

That evening, with his mother at work, Billy sat on the sofa, radio off, books closed. His mind was locked to the thing he had done. His thoughts seemed to take something to his chest, which was the one part of his body that felt different from before. He didn't feel pain, but a kind of pressure that caused him often to sigh and breathe out, as if to relieve himself of the burden that came to rest near the heart of his body.

He sat and simply waited to become sleepy enough for bed. More than anything, he wanted sleep. It was the only thing he could do to escape, for a time, what he had brought to himself.

*****

Mrs. Roarke opened the door. "Mrs. Pearson. Please come in."

"Hello, Mrs. Roarke."

"Can I get you a cup of tea? Please have a seat."

"No, nothing to drink, thank you. I appreciate your allowing me to speak with Billy before he leaves for military school."

"Yes, of course. Please have a seat. I'll tell him you're here."

Billy entered the parlor and stood near the sofa where his teacher sat. An initial smile faded as he dropped his head and stared at the floor. "Hello, Mrs. Pearson."

"Hello, Billy."

"If you'll excuse me, Mrs. Pearson, I'll leave the two of you to speak in private."

"Thank you."

Billy remained standing, but slowly raised his head to meet his teacher's stare. There was a tone to her face that was serious, though it could not mask her natural kindness. Mrs. Pearson did not smile – didn't come close to it – but her presence was comforting to him.

"Please sit down, Billy. I came here because I wanted to speak with you before you left for school."

"Yes, thank you."

"I can't pretend that I wasn't deeply hurt by what you did to Thomas. Thank God he is going to be fine. Thomas is a wonderful young boy, with a very kind and sensitive heart, and he did not deserve what you did to him."

Billy sat with his back leaning forward, his arms resting on his legs, his eyes becoming wet. "I know, Mrs. Pearson." He talked and cried at the same time, his words interrupted by sobs and sniffles. "I'm so . . . sorry . . . I can't believe . . . I did that . . . to him. I hope God punishes me . . . real bad."

Billy began to cry hard and steady, unhindered by words. Mrs. Pearson handed him a fresh handkerchief. He blew his nose and thanked her. The two of them sat without speaking as he gradually grew calmer.

"Billy, we live in a wonderful world," she said after some time, "but it is not a perfect one. And sometimes very bad things happen. What we have to do is learn from the bad things. You are responsible for what happened to Thomas. You are also responsible for how you live your life from now on. If you are truly sorry for what you've done, you will allow this unfortunate incident to make you a better person."

"Yes, Mrs. Pearson."

"I've written down my address for you. If you'd like, you may write me from military school. I'd like to hear how you're getting along."

"I'll write you." He took her address and placed the small slip of paper in his shirt pocket.

"Good. Now could you tell your mother that I'm ready to leave?"

He found his mother in her bedroom and told her his teacher was leaving. She said nothing to him, got up from her chair and walked past him to the parlor.

"Thank you, Mrs. Pearson, for coming," she said. "It was very kind of you to say goodbye."

"It was my pleasure. Your son has always been very dear to me."

Mrs. Roarke said nothing.

Mrs. Pearson left and Mrs. Roarke closed the front door. Nothing was said as she and her son returned to their bedrooms and shut the doors behind them.

The next afternoon, his mother entered Billy's bedroom without a knock. "Randall and Charlie are here. You have ten minutes to talk to them outside, if you wish."

"Yes, Mom." He sat up and set down his book.

"I have to talk outside," he said to his friends when he got to the door. The boys walked slowly and silently, and sat on the curb.

"Hey, Billy," Randall said at last, "I can't believe we finally got to talk to ya. Your mom said every day you weren't allowed to come out and talk."

"I know."

"What's going to happen, Billy? Where are you going to go to school?" Charlie asked.

"I'm going to military school."

"Military school?" Randall said. "Is this on the level? What I wouldn't give to get to go to military school. You gonna get a gun?"

"No. I don't know."

"Where?" Charlie asked. "Where's the school?"

"It's about five miles that way." Billy pointed to the mountains. "It's in Altadena. It's called Eagleton Military Academy for Boys. I have to live there."

"Live there? Billy," Randall said, "what a break."

Billy looked at Randall and wondered how anyone could think living away from home would be any kind of break.

"I'll miss you," Charlie said.

"Oh yeah, I'll miss ya," Randall said, "but you're gonna get to shoot guns n' play war 'n' wear a uniform. My cousin Freddie used to go to military school. He said he got to shoot people with real bullets. And he got to go on patrols and sleep in the mud."

"I'm not going to shoot anybody."

"Don't say that, Billy. You never know."

"When do you get to come home?" Charlie asked.

"My mom said I can come home on the weekends."

"Is your mother still mad at you?" Charlie asked.

"Yeah, I think so. Yeah, she's still mad."

"Ah, your ol' lady's not the kind to stay sore forever," Randall said. "I think she's calmin' down. We've been knockin' on your door every day for a week, ever since you beat . . . uh . . . and every day she seemed not as sore as the day before. Right, Charlie?"

"Right. We were kind of afraid to come over, but today she was almost nice about it."

"Well," Billy replied, "I think she's starting to get worried. I heard her on the telephone today. She kept asking the school about polio. She's afraid I might get polio living with other boys."

"My mom's afraid I'll get polio, too," Charlie said. "That's why I'm not allowed to go swimming."

"So whatd'ya know about this Eagleson joint?" Randall asked.

"Eagleton. Not much. I have to wear a uniform. I go to class. I live in a barracks. I don't know much else."

"No lousy girls," Randall said. "Now that's a school for me. How do I join up?"

"Ask your mom. It's seventy-five dollars a month."

"Aw, tough break. We ain't got that kinda dough."

"So, how's school? Mrs. Pearson came to visit me yesterday."

"Oh, yeah?" Randall replied. "She didn't tell us. She hasn't said much about you. Only that you got expelled. Thomas came back to school a couple days ago. A big hero. Like he was wounded in the war or somethin'. I don't talk to him, though."

Billy didn't respond.

"When do you start military school?" Charlie asked.

"Monday. I have to go Monday."

"Boy, oh boy, Billy," Randall said. "This didn't turn out bad for you at all. Ya get to go to military school. You're lucky, pal. You sure are lucky."

CHAPTER

Ten

A taxi brought Billy and his mother to Eagleton on Monday afternoon. They sat separated in the back seat by a footlocker, a large case that held Billy's belongings: towels, underwear, socks, play clothes, toothbrush, soap, comb, books, baseball and mitt.

Billy wore his new school uniform, which his mother had arranged for him to get before he arrived. He thought it was a sharp-looking outfit, but that it wasn't something he wanted to wear every day. The recipe for a properly dressed Eagleton cadet included a black tie tucked halfway down a white shirt, dark grey pants and a dark grey coat with gold buttons. A wide black belt with a brass buckle wrapped around the coat, keeping everything tight and trim. A two-cornered hat sat atop Billy's head, while shiny black shoes hung in the air, not yet able to reach the floor.

The taxi parked at the school entrance. Mrs. Roarke asked the cabbie to wait for her as he helped Billy with his footlocker.

The front gate was tall and made of black iron. It was framed by two columns of round stones painted white. Mrs. Roarke had been here before, but stopped as she and Billy entered the grounds so that he could look around.

The school was spread out, not concentrated in one building like Wilson. An asphalt lot was ahead of them, beyond which a short flight of steps led to a large grass field. Rising beyond the field were the blue San Gabriel Mountains. To the right were small wooden buildings that looked like classrooms, painted white with green roofs. To the left was a large rectangular garden – planted with bushes, shrubs and trees – that was bordered on all sides by a wide walkway. A wooden trellis, supporting flowered vines, covered the entire perimeter of the walkway.

Surrounding this courtyard stood white stucco buildings with red tile roofs. Most of these buildings were barracks, living quarters for the cadets. Mrs. Roarke led Billy to the first building, which included the office of Eagleton's commandant, Major William Chandler.

Billy left his footlocker outside the door as he and his mother stepped inside. A secretary knowingly greeted Mrs. Roarke and offered both of them a chair, adding that the major would see them shortly.

Billy and his mother had not spoken to each other during the taxi ride to school. She did not appear to be angry with him anymore, but seemed anxious. She had been very concerned about Thomas and what her son did, but during the last few days, when the arrangements for military school were made and Billy's situation became clear, she began to think only of him.

After a short wait, Major Chandler emerged from his office. "Mrs. Roarke," he said, carrying the tone of an old friend, "how good to see you again. Forgive me for keeping you."

"That's quite all right, Major," she replied with a faint smile as she stood to shake his hand. She then sent her arm in the direction of her son. "This, Major Chandler, is Billy."

He stood as the major bent forward to greet him with a warm smile. "Welcome to Eagleton, Billy. Now, shall we sit in my office and chat for a bit?"

Billy thought the commandant looked like someone's grandpa in a uniform. He thought he was nice, but wondered if, like some adults, he was nice only because his mother was with him.

The walls of Major Chandler's office were covered with photographs, mostly of cadets and classes from previous years at Eagleton. There was a bookshelf filled with yearbooks and history books. On the wall behind the commandant's desk hung two swords and a diploma from West Point. A window by the desk viewed the courtyard.

Major Chandler offered seats to Mrs. Roarke and Billy, then sat down behind his desk.

"You really have quite a lovely school, Major," Mrs. Roarke said, looking through the window.

"Thank you. We pride ourselves on maintaining a good appearance." The commandant folded his hands on his desk and moved forward. "Mrs. Roarke, I know you had many concerns and questions about Eagleton. I want you to know that we will always have your boy's best interests in mind. If at any time you should have any further questions or concerns, please know that you can call us anytime. Our job here is to build good Americans, and you play a great part in that."

"Thank you, Major. Thank you so much." She took a handkerchief from her purse and wiped her eyes.

The commandant turned to Billy. "Now, how about you, young man? Is there anything you'd like to ask me?"

Billy had so many questions he didn't know which ones to ask. He was also suspicious. He didn't want to be too friendly with the major, only to find him different after his mother left.

"Uh, no, sir. Not right now anyway."

"Well, that's fine. I will tell you, Billy, that there are many things to learn, but we will give you time. You and our other younger cadets, the sixth and seventh graders, are what we call the junior school, and we ease up a bit on those young fellows. And . . . oh yes, it almost slipped my mind. I want to introduce you to your barracks leader, Cadet Lieutenant Mitchell. Pardon me."

The commandant stepped into a neighboring room, then returned shortly to his seat. "He'll arrive in a moment."

"How old is Lieutenant Mitchell?" Mrs. Roarke asked.

The commandant looked up, as if to gain the answer from above. "Mitchell is . . . I believe . . . fourteen or fifteen. He is in tenth grade. One of our finest cadets. Ah, here he is."

Lieutenant Mitchell entered the room. He was tall and thin with greasy hair and pimples, but possessed a sober confidence. He carried more medals on his uniform than did Major Chandler.

"Lieutenant, I would like to introduce you to your newest cadet, Private Billy Roarke. And this is his mother."

Lieutenant Mitchell dropped his head and shook hands with Billy's mother. "It's a pleasure, ma'am."

She nodded. "How do you do, Lieutenant?"

Lieutenant Mitchell looked at the commandant. "Private Roarke seems like a fine addition to our barracks, sir. I look forward to working with him."

"Fine. Keep in mind that this is his first time in a military school. Go easy for a spell. No demerits for not saluting an officer, or any other such transgressions, until he has been properly instructed."

"Yes, sir."

"Dismissed."

The lieutenant saluted Major Chandler, then turned to Mrs. Roarke and nodded. "Ma'am." He then turned to Billy. "Private."

After he left the office, Mrs. Roarke said nervously, "He seems very mature, but . . . now he is in charge of the barracks where Billy will live? Is that right?"

"Yes, Mrs. Roarke. However, adult officers and staff members have ultimate authority over all cadets. Our young boys, including the officers, are closely supervised. We hold a tight rein."

She sighed. "Well, I don't believe I have any more questions, Major. Perhaps I should be going."

She stood to shake the commandant's hand and he tried one last time to lessen her anxiety. "Don't worry, Mrs. Roarke. We will take good care of your boy. That is our job."

"Thank you, Major Chandler."

The commandant nodded, then looked at Billy. "Private Roarke, you are quartered in Barracks C, just down the corridor a bit."

Billy said goodbye to the major and left the building with his mother. Together, they stood by the footlocker he had set by the door.

She held his shoulders and breathed heavily. "Billy, sweetheart, please be safe here."

"I will, Mom."

"And please be a good boy."

"I will. Don't cry. I'll be home Friday, remember?"

She nodded and held her handkerchief to her moist face.

"Okay, Mom. You better go now. The cab is waiting. I'll be all right. And I'll be good. Everything's going to be fine."

Her face showed that she wasn't sure. She bent down and kissed her son on the cheek, then left him. Billy lifted the footlocker and walked down the corridor, looking for his new home.

He gratefully released the burden of the trunk as he found a door labeled "Barracks C." He switched the footlocker to his left hand, opened the door and stepped inside.

The big echoing sounds of shouting boys bouncing off the concrete floor and white walls, sinks and toilets of the barracks latrine, snapped Billy's eyes wide open and forced him to stand frozen in place. Three boys were dragging another on his back across the damp floor to an open shower stall near where Billy stood. Clad only in white underwear, the jumble of flesh moved at the stuttered pace guaranteed by conflicting purpose and an unsure surface.

"Noooo! Don't!" the besieged boy cried as the group entered the shower stall.

"Too late, Lyle. We warned you. You're a pig and you're going to pay," one boy said as he tried to lift Lyle from his seated position on the shower floor.

"Where's the Old Dutch?" the tallest one in the group asked. He was a dark-haired, muscular boy named Roberts, who looked a year or two older than the rest. "Come on! Where's the stuff?"

"It's by the sink," one said as they struggled to keep the squirming boy from leaving the shower.

"Hey, you," Roberts said to Billy, finally acknowledging the stranger. "Get the Old Dutch and the brush over there, will ya?"

"Uh, no," he replied, without much confidence. "Why don't you leave him alone?"

"Forget it. Canfield, get the stuff. I'll hold both his legs."

Canfield left the shower stall and slipped and fell in the middle of his short trip to recover the jar of cleanser and the stiff wooden brush. On his way back, he looked at Billy. "Thanks for nothin', pal."

Billy continued to look on in uncomfortable silence.

"Okay, pour it on," Roberts said.

Canfield vigorously shook the can of Old Dutch above the boy. A cloud of cleanser dust began to fog the stall.

"Okay, start brushing. Wait, give *me* the brush," Roberts ordered. He began to scrape the boy's skin and hair with the rough bristles. "All right, turn on the water."

The water streamed down, clearing the air, but adding to the sounds of mayhem already filling the large latrine.

Lyle now lay on his right side. His knees were pulled up to his chest, and his hands and arms covered his head, as he now tried to protect his body rather than break free.

"Listen, Lyle," Roberts said as he continued to brush the boy's skin, "we warned you. We told you, you were gettin' a G.I. shower if you didn't clean yourself. You're a disgrace to the barracks, Lyle. You smell, your bunk smells, and we're sick 'n' tired of it. Do you understand now?"

Lyle screamed, "Ahhh!. . . I hate you!"

"Ow! Ow! The water's hot! Turn it off! *Turn it off!*" Roberts shouted as he jumped up and out of the way of the stream that had largely fallen on his back.

Canfield turned the water off. "Sorry, Rob."

"You burned my back, Canfield! Get out of here! C'mon, everybody outta here!"

The three boys looked like a defeated army in retreat as they left the latrine in silence, not one of them looking at Billy.

Billy turned to Lyle, who was working to get up from the shower floor. "Here, let me help you," he said as he offered his hand.

"Get out of here!" he shouted. "You're just as big a jerk as they are! Don't touch me!"

Lyle stood and turned on the shower. He adjusted the handles for a pleasant temperature and stood under the spray, rinsing the caustic white residue from his scratched, red skin.

Billy wanted to cry. He wanted to see his mother. He wanted to be home. He hated this place. He hated everything and everybody in it. He wondered how he could have ended up in a place like this. Then he thought of his father and wondered where he was, what kind of place he was in. He wondered if he was scared and lonely, too. They were all separated now. His father away at war. His mother at home. And here he was in military school. He realized now that he truly hated the war. He hated the war for what it had done to him. He hated the war for what it had done to his family.

CHAPTER

Eleven

Billy used his footlocker to push himself through a swing-ing door that led to his new home, Barracks C. The room was large. Metal frame beds, supporting thin narrow mattresses dressed in dark blue blankets, were parked perpendicular against pale green walls. The wooden floor was old and splin-tery, and only the wall facing the courtyard had windows.

Several boys were at their bunks, engaged in personal maintenance chores: polishing shoes and belt buckles, fold-ing clothes. The gang that carried Lyle to the shower was get-ting dried and dressed.

Billy stood in the large open center of the barracks and observed his new world. He wondered how so many boys could live together in such a room. Not having any brothers or sisters, he had never even shared a house with another child. How in the world, he thought to himself, was he going to live in a barracks with twenty other boys?

Billy was afraid to ask anyone for help, but he didn't know which bed was his, and he began to feel peculiar standing alone in the wide open space.

Help arrived in the form of a young cadet, who had been lying on his bunk reading a book.

"Hey, partner," the boy called from his bed, as he set his book down and sat up, "you the new one?"

"Yes."

"You're here next to me."

Billy walked to the bunk closest to the latrine door and set his footlocker on the bed.

"I'm Gilbert," the boy said, now standing. They shook hands.

"I'm Billy. Nice to meet you."

"Pleasure's mine. They told me you were coming and to show you the ropes till you get comfortable."

Billy was scared. He was still feeling the shock and the sadness that the scene in the latrine had brought him.

"Cheer up, old boy," Gilbert said. "This place ain't so bad. It has its irritating qualities, but I'll help you through."

"Thanks."

"You a seventh grader?"

"Yeah. Yes. I'm in seventh grade," Billy said, as if he didn't remember.

"So am I. We've got the Colonel."

"The Colonel?"

"Our teacher. Was discharged last year from the army. No one knows why for sure. There's a million rumors going around, but they can't all be true."

"What kind of rumors?"

"Oh, all sorts o' stuff. A lot of people say he socked Ol' Patton right in the kisser. Hazelnut says he cursed Ike. Hillier says he drove a tank through the White House. Crazy stuff."

"What do you think?"

"I believe the Patton one. That sounds like the Colonel. So, what are you in for?"

"Oh . . . I got in some trouble at my school," he said softly.

"Hey, no need to spill your guts now. By the way, what's your last name? We call each other by our last names around here."

"Roarke."

"Okay, Roarke. Well, my *first* name is John, like the actor. John Gilbert."

"So why are you here?" Billy asked as he undid the latch on his footlocker and started to unpack.

"I'm here 'cause my parents have a lot o' dough, if you want to know the truth."

"Where do you live?"

"San Marino."

"Oh. I live in Pasadena."

"Well, that makes us neighbors. Hey, you're a reader." Gilbert watched Billy drop a copy of *A Connecticut Yankee in King Arthur's Court* on his bed. "Mark Twain. He's a swell writer. Funny and good. A lot of the great writers aren't funny."

"Yeah, I like him, too."

"I read a lot of Dickens around here. All that horrific boarding school stuff. You know, 'Please, sir, may I have more porridge?' It makes this place look like the Biltmore Hotel."

Lyle now entered the barracks, leaving wet footprints on the wooden floor.

"There goes a pathetic creature," Gilbert said.

"I saw what they did to him in the shower."

"Oh, yeah. Sheriff Rob and his posse delivering justice for the citizens of Barracks C."

"How old is that guy Rob?"

"He's thirty-two years old. He's in the eighth grade, but he's about thirty-two."

Billy laughed for the first time in many days.

"Don't worry. I won't give you all the fascinating details of this place all at once. I'll guide you through gradually."

"Thanks," he said as he started stacking clothes on his bed.

"One thing, though, Roarke. As you can see, there're no dressers here, so no need to unpack that stuff. It all stays in your footlocker under your bed."

"Oh, yeah, right."

"Speaking of which, the footlocker must be exactly in the middle under your bunk. If it's not there during inspection, you'll find your belongings thrown all over the barracks, including the latrine."

"How often is inspection?"

"Only every morning when we're in class. And I'll show you how to make your bed so that a dime bounces from the blanket. They love to see that dime bounce, boy. If it doesn't, your bedding goes bye-bye, too."

Billy sighed. He felt like he was becoming sick.

"Hey, cheer up. I'm telling you all the horrible stuff. There's good things about this place."

"Oh?"

"Sure. But it's not the food. I hope you're not one for food. I am and it's tough. Every single night I go to bed thinking about food. Last night I was thinking about a steak covered with mushroom gravy before I finally dozed off. One night I had an actual dream that I was eating liver and onions. And I hate liver and onions."

Billy grimaced. "Oooh. I like food, too. I was hoping it was going to be good. I guess I won't be eating much during the week."

"Oh, you'll eat all right. They don't let you leave the mess hall until your tray is clean as a whistle. They make you eat *everything*."

"What if you don't?"

"They think of interesting things for you to do. Trust me, you'll eat the food."

Roberts, on his way to the latrine, stopped at Billy's bunk. "Who's this?" he asked Gilbert.

"Your newest subject, your highness. Private Roarke. A fine lad, who showers regularly."

"You're screwy, Gilbert."

"Thank you, sire."

Roberts entered the latrine with a shaking head and rolled up eyes.

"Roarke," Gilbert said as he put a hand on Billy's shoulder, "you look horrible. Don't worry about all this. Like I said, there's good things about this place."

"Like what?"

"I'll tell you at dinner. It'll take your mind off the food."

CHAPTER
Twelve

Lieutenant Mitchell emerged from the recessed corner of the barracks where he was quartered. "Fall in, Barracks C," he ordered. "Dinner. Fall in."

Gilbert nudged Billy, who was lying on his bunk reading. "C'mon, Roarke. We've got to line up for dinner."

The cadets assembled in three lines on the corridor outside their barracks, standing at attention and facing the lush garden courtyard and Lieutenant Mitchell, who gave the orders "Left Face," then "Forward March."

Billy didn't know how to properly execute a "Left Face" command, but he did manage to turn left and stay somewhat in step with the barracks.

The cadets marched to the asphalt lot in front of the mess hall and stood at a silent attention, along with the rest of the school. Facing them were three cadet officers, including the battalion commander. Behind them casually stood Major Chandler.

The BC studied the platoons and excused them to dinner one at a time, according to how quiet and still they were.

Roberts stood behind Billy and whispered, "Don't move, new kid. I'm hungry." Billy tried to become straighter than he already was.

Gilbert, who was behind Roberts, heard this and whispered, "Don't move, Rob. There's a wasp on your back."

"Get it off me," he replied with closed lips.

"I can't. You know we're not allowed to move. He's crawling up your collar now. He's about to go down your neck."

Roberts began slapping the back of his neck, causing Lieutenant Mitchell to turn and investigate the unrhythmic percussion sounds coming from his platoon.

Roberts got stung with five demerits and the platoon remained outside until all the others had entered the mess hall.

Billy didn't like the smell of the mess hall kitchen. It had a steamy, unidentifiable odor, not the pleasant aroma of good things roasting and baking. He grabbed a tray and utensils, and walked down the line, waiting his turn for workers to slap him his servings.

"Hey, Leonard," Roberts said to the head cook, a middle-aged black man dressed in white, "gimme somethin' good tonight. I don't like this stuff."

Leonard didn't respond.

Billy received a thick puddle of brown stew which filled the largest compartment of his tray. He thought there was no way something that looked that bad could taste good, but he said thank you anyway.

"You're welcome," Leonard replied.

Next down the line, a pale-skinned man called Smitty served applesauce while an unlit, half-smoked cigarette balanced from his lower lip.

Billy said thank you again, but Smitty did not respond, perhaps in fear of unseating his cigarette.

Billy grabbed a slice of bread and a glass of milk, and walked into the mess hall: a large room filled with long wooden tables set apart like rungs on a ladder. He stood and waited for Gilbert, then together they sat at a table with some of Gilbert's friends.

"Maglioni, Hazelnut, this is Roarke," Gilbert said, "the newest resident of Barracks C."

"Hi," Maglioni said. "I saw you before."

"Why are you starting school so late?" Hazelnut asked. "It's already February."

"Well . . ."

"Don't be so nosy, 'Nut," Gilbert said. "Try to make a guy feel welcome."

"I don't know how he'd feel welcome eating this slop. Yuck."

"Boy, I'll say," Gilbert said. "This dish is particularly repulsive. Now listen, Roarke." He continued in a hushed tone. "That lieutenant at the end there is the table officer. He makes sure you eat everything and that you don't play with your food – all the fun stuff."

"Thanks for the warning."

"No sweat."

"This can't be beef," Hazelnut said, poking his food.

"Maybe not," Gilbert said, "but this place could ruin a porterhouse steak. I don't know *what* this stuff is. I can identify a carrot . . . oh, and here's a pea. I don't know, it's just unidentifiable morsels held together in a brown glue."

"The applesauce isn't bad," Billy said.

"No, Roarke!" Gilbert cried. "You've got to save the applesauce for the end. You don't want to leave here with the taste of the brown glue in your mouth. And make sure you have some bread with each bite of stew."

"And it helps if you don't breathe," Maglioni said.

He took the advice and ate the stew, followed with a bite of bread, all the while trying not to breathe.

"I'll just hold my nose," Billy said, finding it hard to follow Maglioni's tip.

"You can't, Roarke," Gilbert said. "Table officers frown on that."

"Oh, swell. So *what* is it that's good about this place?"

"Well," Gilbert replied, "what's good about it is that . . . it's really not as bad as it seems."

"That's it?"

"The commandant's nice," Maglioni said.

"Yeah, so what?" Hazelnut said. "We never deal with him anyway. We've got to deal with Mitchell and that lunatic, the Colonel. Are you in seventh grade, Roarke?"

"Yeah."

"Tough luck."

"How bad is this 'Colonel' teacher?" Billy asked after wincing from a bite of stew.

"He's really not so bad."

"Oh, sure, Gilbert," Hazelnut said. "Not for you, since you're the teacher's pet. You're the only one he doesn't destroy every time you open your mouth."

"Oh, brother," Billy said. "He sounds rough."

"You're lucky," Hazelnut said. "You only get him for half the year. We'll have him for the whole year."

"What do you think?" Billy asked Maglioni. "Is he really that bad?"

Maglioni paused before speaking. "Let me put it this way. The Army kicks him out for slugging General Patton, 'Ol'

Blood 'n' Guts' himself. The Army thinks he's too tough for *Patton*. So *we* get him. Yeah, I'm sorry to break it to you. He's not a nice teacher."

After dinner, Eagleton cadets were given a half hour free period in their barracks before attending study hall in their classrooms. Study hall in Billy's class was supervised by Mr. Tredwiller, a skinny man whose job it was to help cadets with their homework.

Mr. Tredwiller, however, never spoke. He sat at the teacher's desk with his head down, working on projects from his day job as an accountant for a department store.

Billy sat in the back of the room, with no homework assignment, and wondered if he should introduce himself to the man.

As he rose, Gilbert handed him a hastily written note.

> *"Roarke – Sorry I forgot to warn you.*
> *Don't talk to him. Tredwiller gives 5*
> *demerits for each syllable spoken in*
> *class. I'll give you my book."*

Gilbert gave him his copy of *Bleak House* and started his homework. Billy began reading, lifting his head to observe Mr. Tredwiller every so often. Each time the man was the same, as if Billy were looking at a photograph. At eight-thirty, after an hour and a half of silence, the cadets, on their own, left the classroom. Mr. Tredwiller, head down, continued his work.

Lights out was at nine o'clock. The bugle blew taps as Billy lay in his bunk and thought about what had brought him to

74

this bed. A few minutes of violence that led to, at least, months of this. Billy now wished that Thomas had hit him back, had hurt him. Wished that he had made a fight of it. Why did Thomas just take it? Was Billy that strong, that powerful?

He had never fought like that before. He had never been angry like that before. There was something in him that emerged that day that had lain still within him all his young life, like a comet streaking hot and white, seen once in a lifetime. Did it leave him that day, or did remnants of the blast remain within him?

Whatever it was, Billy did not understand it. He only understood that what he had done had brought him here. And though his first day at military school was not a full one, it contained more than enough nastiness to confirm that Billy did get his wish. God was punishing him real bad.

CHAPTER

Thirteen

Billy's first morning at Eagleton began like all the rest would. The bugle blew reveille at six o'clock, always waking the boys before they wished. The latrine soon became a traffic jam of youngsters maneuvering to splash their faces, rinse their mouths and use the toilets. Billy waited his turn more politely than others. He found his new bathroom arrangements very unpleasant.

Back at his bunk he dressed himself in his new uniform, while Gilbert showed him how to make a snappy Windsor knot for his tie.

He made his bed, taking his time and trying to do a good job. Gilbert looked at the finished product and frowned. "That won't do, my friend."

"It's not good enough?"

Gilbert took a coin from his footlocker and flipped it onto Billy's bed. "There's no bounce, Roarke. See? Now, look at my bunk." Gilbert tossed the dime onto his own bed and saw it spring back into the air as if his blanket were a trampoline. "Now that's the bounce you want."

Gilbert tore off Billy's blanket and sheets, and demonstrated the way to dress the mattress so that it would provide the desired lift.

"Okay," Gilbert said as he again flipped the dime on Billy's bunk. "There you go. That's what you want. The key is stretching everything very tight. You'll get the hang of it."

"Thanks. Thanks a lot."

"No sweat."

After making their bunks, the cadets set themselves to the task of cleaning the barracks and latrine.

"Our side has the barracks this week," Gilbert said. "It's a better duty than the latrine. I'll get us a broom and dustpan, and we can sweep."

All the cadets worked. Some swept; some dusted the radiators and window sills; some mopped the latrine floor; some cleaned showers, sinks and toilets.

Lieutenant Mitchell supervised the activity, walking around, inspecting and admonishing. "Get that spider web in the corner ceiling, Priedler. And make sure you kill the spider. A dead spider makes no webs."

"How do I reach it, sir?"

"Stand on a bunk and use your broom. Think, Priedler."

At times, Lieutenant Mitchell addressed all the cadets. "Let's go, Barracks C. I want a spotless barracks, spic 'n' span. I want to win 'Honor Barracks' this year. Do you want the same, Barracks C?"

"Yes, sir," they said.

"What did you say?"

"Yes, sir!" they yelled.

"Private Priedler," Lieutenant Mitchell said, "where is the dead spider?"

"I can't find it, sir. I think I smashed it."

"Then bring me his legs. A spider has eight legs. You will receive one demerit for each leg you don't find."

"Yes, sir."

"And be glad I didn't have you look for a centipede."

"Yes, sir."

Lieutenant Mitchell moved over to Billy. "Private Roarke, you are too slow with that broom. You're not in your easy little public school anymore. Sweep faster."

"Yes, sir."

"Sir," Priedler said, "I found his legs. I got all eight of them."

"Where is the body, Priedler?"

"I can't find it, sir, but I don't think he can make a web without legs."

Mitchell looked at the legs Priedler held in his hand. "Nice work, Private."

"Thank you, sir."

"And now," the lieutenant began pulling hair from Priedler's eyebrows, "we have found the centipede."

"Uh, yes, sir. Sorry, sir."

"You have twenty-five demerits, Private. You will march them off during free time. And give me twenty right now."

"Yes, sir." Priedler dropped to the floor and started the push-ups. "One, sir; two, sir; three, sir . . ."

"Start again, Private. Your buckle is not touching the floor, and your back is not straight."

"Yes, sir. One, sir; two, sir . . ."

Breakfast was better than dinner, although there was something in the oatmeal which some boys thought were large raisins and others thought were small prunes. No one was sure what they were eating, but like everything else on their tray, they had to eat it.

Billy watched one boy furtively bring his tray below the table, then return it with the oatmeal missing. When the table officer checked his tray, he noticed a glob of the mystery fruit oatmeal sitting on one of his shoes. The cadet was given many demerits and ordered to mop the entire mess hall floor after drill.

Eagleton cadets drilled for one hour each weekday after breakfast. Billy marched with his barracks platoon, who along with two other platoons, formed Company D, which was led by the company commander, Cadet Lieutenant Mitchell.

Billy found the first day of drill confusing. He didn't know what "Column Left" or "Right Flank" meant, and sometimes turned left when he shouldn't have and sometimes walked straight when he shouldn't have.

In addition, he didn't think Lieutenant Mitchell spoke clearly when he gave orders during drill. His "Left" command sounded like "Layef," and "Right" sounded like "Righoo." And he had no idea how "Forward March" became "Forward Hoo." But it did.

Billy did enjoy the marching chants led by Lieutenant Mitchell.

> *"We're going to march to Berlin tonight.*
> *Layef . . . layef.*
> *We're gonna kick Hitler in the head, all right.*
> *Layef . . . layef."*

He was sure Lieutenant Mitchell made up these chants, because he had so many. Most of them were about beating up Hitler.

After drill the cadets marched back to their barracks, and Billy lay on his bunk. In a few minutes they would march to their classroom. Billy had never done so much before eight-thirty in the morning. He felt like he'd already had a full day and he wasn't even in class yet. Lieutenant Mitchell was right. He wasn't in his easy little public school anymore.

The students' straight line collapsed as they entered their classroom, each cadet walking in rigid silence to his desk. Billy waited until the others filled their places, then nervously, as if he were late for church, seated himself in the lone empty desk located in the middle of the front row. Stationed directly in front of him stood a man facing the blackboard, inspecting what he had just written. The man accurately tossed a small piece of white chalk onto the blackboard tray, blew a quick burst of air onto his fingers, then swung his body swiftly and smoothly to meet the reverent stares of his students. The man wore a coat and tie, but on him it looked like a uniform.

He was a lesson in geometry. His light brown crew cut created a flat plane on top of a head shaped like a block of granite. The back of his skull did not curve, but connected with his neck in a straight line. His jaw, square and strong, provided a firm foundation for his facial features: a thin, straight mouth, and a nose that projected at a 45-degree angle from the center of two thin, gray eyes. His neck was a perfect cylinder, and his strong chest and narrow waist suggested a triangle. The only deviation from this model of manhood was the dark wooden cane the man held in his left hand. He leaned on his right foot and used this cane to tap the top of Billy's desk.

"What's your name, Private?" he said in a sure and mighty voice that matched his appearance.

"Billy, sir."

"Billy? What's your last name, Private?"

"Roarke, sir. My name's Billy Roarke. I'm new."

The man's eyebrows let Billy know that the last bit of information he revealed was quite unnecessary.

"Well, Roarke, let me attempt to equal your sterling introduction. I am Mr. Charles Hollenbeck. You will call me 'sir.' I am not about to waste my time regurgitating all the regulations and code I've already stated to this class, so you will either have to find a cadet here to bring you up to snuff on my standards and practices, or through your own observations use your God-given gifts of reason, logic and intelligence to determine what is expected. In your case, I suggest the former."

"Yes, sir."

"Yes, sir. That's a good start, Roarke," he said with sarcasm.

The Colonel did not move from his spot in front of the class as he began the lesson. "Cadets, as you can see, the question of the day is this: 'Who is the greatest general in the history of the world?' And by general, I include all supreme military leaders whose title might be otherwise."

The cadets sat in silence, thinking without answering. Billy thought of George Washington, but was in no mood to speak.

"Let's demonstrate our hospitality," the Colonel said, "by beginning with our newest cadet. Private Roarke, what say you in response to the question of the day?"

"Uhm . . . I don't . . ."

"Stand, Private. Cadets do not speak in this class while seated. You must stand at attention when called upon."

Billy stood. "Yes, sir."

"Your response, Private."

"I don't know, sir."

"You don't know, Private Roarke? You don't have sufficient knowledge of the world which you inhabit, or you haven't given sufficient thought to the traumas of time that would lead you to develop that most human of traits – an opinion?"

"I just don't know, sir."

"A sparkling start, Private. Sit down."

"Yes, sir."

The Colonel turned to another cadet. "Private Sanders, inspire us."

Private Sanders rose to attention. "I believe Hannibal was the greatest general, sir. The Carthaginian who . . ."

"I know who Hannibal was, Private. Give me your reasons, not your schoolbook facts."

"Well, sir, I like the way he managed all those elephants and soldiers over the Alps in order to attack Rome."

"Did Hannibal defeat Rome, Private?"

"No, sir."

"Then you recommend him quite well as Supreme Circus Trainer. Sit down."

"Yes, sir."

"Corporal Mason, respond."

"I choose William the Conqueror, sir," the corporal said as he stood at attention. "I believe he changed history with his invasion of England."

"Changing history is an idiotic reason for choosing greatness, Corporal. History has no course but change and is often orchestrated by idiots. Yours is an empty statement. In addition, William's victories were largely a result of the blunders of his foes. A remarkably poor choice."

"Yes, sir."

"Maglioni, respond."

Private Maglioni stood. "I think General Patton is a great general, sir." The class hummed, and Maglioni immediately knew he had erred in naming the man the Colonel is said to have slugged.

The Colonel stared at Maglioni. "Well, Private," he finally said, "will we be privileged to hear your defense of General Patton as the greatest in history, or will we be forced to accept the answer based solely on your first-rate reputation?"

"Well," Maglioni continued nervously, "uh . . . I just think he's won some hard battles for us in the war, sir."

"Thank you, Private Maglioni. Thank you for not forcing me to rethink my opinion of you. Well done."

"Thank you, sir."

"Private Metz, respond."

"Sir," Private Metz said as he rose, "Winston Churchill said that General Rommel was a great general. I think I'll vote for Rommel, sir."

The Colonel sighed. "Private Metz, where do I begin? Firstly, this is not an election. Therefore, you have no vote. I will now ignore several magnificent flaws in your answer and respond to merely the most obvious. Surprising as it is to me, I will agree that Rommel is a competent general. But need I remind you, Private, that he is the enemy. And we will never, Private Metz, give honor and glory to the enemy in this class-room. Is that completely understood?"

"Yes, sir."

"Sit, Private Metz. Corporal Gilbert, save us."

Gilbert stood. "In my opinion, sir, George Washington is the greatest general in history, due to his victory over a vastly superior foe and the fact that his struggle was based on the moral and just cause of freedom and independence."

"An excellent response, Corporal Gilbert, in relation to the nonsense dispensed by your peers. But wrong nonetheless."

"Yes, sir."

"Sit down. The answer, cadets, to the question, 'Who is the greatest general in the history of the world?' is . . . " the Colonel paused, ". . . the general who wins this war. This war is like no other. It will not merely bring about change; it will determine nothing less than the survival of mankind."

The Colonel surveyed the room and saw the quiet fear that had spread across the faces of his young students. "At ease, gentlemen," the Colonel said. "It will be us who wins this war."

CHAPTER

Fourteen

The rest of the day and the rest of the week continued Eagleton's normal schedule. And all through the week Billy waited for one thing: Friday. His mother picked him up that day before dinner and together they took a cab home.

Mrs. Roarke had many questions for Billy, and he answered all of them truthfully, if not completely, avoiding information that he believed would worry her. She learned about Gilbert and the guys, the less than savory food, and his "strict" teacher. She did not learn about the G.I. shower, Priedler's spider or the extent of the Colonel's demeanor.

The conversation continued in the kitchen as Billy sat at the table having crackers and milk while his mother prepared dinner.

"Ham sounds good tonight, Mom. Thanks."

"Well, I saved some ration stamps so you could have a nice meal."

"I could use a nice meal. I'm not kidding about the food at school."

His mother began to offer sympathy, but resisted. "I'm . . . Charlie and Randall were here when I came home from work today. They want to see a movie with you tomorrow."

"Can I go?"

"Yes. I told them you could go."

"Swell. I haven't been to the show in a long time. Any letters from Dad?"

"Oh, yes, on the dining room table."

He retrieved the letter and read it at the kitchen table. "Dad sounds good, but he always sounds like that. Look at this picture he drew for me. It's funny."

His mother turned and looked at the pencil sketch of Mr. Roarke sleeping on his bed. A bubble above him showed him dreaming about throwing a home run pitch to Billy.

"Mom, have you told Dad that I'm in military school?"

"No," she said as she cut potatoes. "I'm not going to tell him about any of this until he comes home. He has enough to trouble himself with." She turned her head to face him. "Don't you think?"

His face turned pink. "Yes, Mom."

Billy savored his dinner, eating well after he was full. He wanted to taste as much delicious food as he could during his weekend leave.

Mrs. Roarke was pleasant that evening and pleased to have her son home. The silent anger she possessed during the time after the beating was gone, and Billy felt relieved to be removed from its oppression. But she remained deeply hurt by what her son had done. She and her husband had taken great care and time to imbue their boy with a strong sense of character and morality. They took him to church. They read to him the great moral tales of literature. They discussed the everyday incidents that visit all children, and together with their son extracted the lessons they taught. Most importantly, Mr. and Mrs. Roarke worked hard at being good people themselves. They were a living example of what they wanted their son to become.

It seemed to be working. Billy was somewhat mischievous at school, at times getting into trouble for minor transgressions, but never for anything like the violence he brought to Thomas.

There were times when Billy appeared to possess an extraordinary amount of character. The proudest moment for his mother remained the time he rescued the baby from the car. She saw in that action the crowning result of her and her husband's work. This was a wonderful boy, she thought. And then he shattered her faith in him. She would now look at him, as she often did this weekend, and try to understand from his face, especially his eyes, what was there deep within that would lead him to such barbarity. She knew that longing for his father was some of it, but she believed that wasn't enough; that alone could not explain it. She had known great sadness as a child, as had many others. It never made them cruel. She looked closely and found nothing. All she saw was the handsome face of the son she loved.

Billy battered two people that Monday afternoon on the school playground. Only one of them had healed.

Billy had a hard time finishing his soda the next day as he, Charlie and Randall sat at the counter at Himmelfarb's waiting for the Saturday matinee. All the questions from Mac and the boys kept him from his treat.

Randall was disappointed to learn that cadets as young as Billy did not use guns at Eagleton. Charlie was disappointed that he couldn't have friends visit him at school; he wanted to see the whole set-up.

Mac was sorry to hear about the bad food and offered to give Billy some candy and sweets to take back with him on Sunday night.

"Thanks, Mac, but they don't let you bring any food from home. Ants."

"Ants? They're afraid o' ants? What kind o' soldiers they makin' if they're afraid o' some lousy little ants?"

"Yeah, Billy," Randall said, "that Eagleson joint don't sound so hot no more. No guns, no food, no fun."

"But, Randall," Charlie said, "no girls, too. Remember?"

"Yeah, now that I can live with."

Mac placed a dish of ice cream in front of another customer, then returned his attention to the boys. "So, what picture you fellas gonna see today?"

"We don't know yet," Billy said. "Either *Ali Baba and the Forty Thieves* or *Sahara*."

"Say, *Sahara's* that war picture with Humphrey Bogart," Mac said. "I love that Humphrey Bogart."

"Yeah," Randall said, "I wanna see that, too, 'cause it's playin' with somethin' called *Dangerous Blondes*. *Ali Baba's* got somethin' with it called *Sing a Jingle* . . . stupid."

"I thought you didn't like girls," Mac said.

"I don't like girls. But I like dangerous blondes."

"I think Billy should decide," Charlie said. "He's had a rough week."

"I vote for *Ali Baba*," Billy said after taking a sip from his soda. "I've seen enough war pictures for awhile."

Billy couldn't escape the war. The show began with newsreels showing the Allies advancing in Italy and the Marines fighting in the Marshall Islands. The cartoon showed Donald

Duck making fun of Hitler. Then previews of coming features were for more war films. All this before *Ali Baba*, the main feature.

After the show the three boys stood outside the theater looking at the poster for the next week's film, *Destination Tokyo*.

"You fellas wanna see this?" Charlie asked.

Randall turned his head toward the street. "Well, would ya get a load o'that."

"What?" Billy asked, still looking at the poster.

"Aw, nothin'."

Billy and Charlie turned and saw two boys walking down the sidewalk. One of them was Thomas.

"Hey, Billy," Charlie said, "why don't you go and apologize to Thomas. Get it off your chest."

"Don't listen to him, Billy. Charlie, are you crazy? That was a fair fight. Billy here didn't fight him dirty. Didn't sneak up on him, didn't kick him. Nothin' but his fists. Fought him like a man." Randall turned to Billy. "You got nothin' to apologize for, pal. It's not your fault Thomas can't fight."

Billy stood still and quiet, staring downward with a face that looked confused and scared.

"I'll go with you, Billy," Charlie said. "C'mon, you'll feel better."

"Billy feels fine, don't ya, pal?" Randall put an arm around Billy and softened his voice. "You fought for your ol' man. He'd be proud o' you. Whatd'ya say?"

"Nothing," Billy said. "I've got nothing to say. Let's go home."

Billy could not enjoy the next day. No matter what he did, Sunday would end with him at school. Even Friday had been a happier day for him, a day in which he woke up in the barracks, marched, ate bad food, endured the Colonel. Friday was better, because the night saw him sleeping in his own bed. Where the day would lead him, its final destination, was most important. Sunday led to Eagleton.

CHAPTER

Fifteen

Monday's lunch was macaroni. Not macaroni with sauce or cheese or meat or butter. Just macaroni, served with boiled spinach and tapioca pudding. Billy and his friends sat together and inspected their meal before eating.

"How do ya like that?" Hazelnut said. "The food here gets lousier every day. Leonard used to put chopped up hot dogs in this stuff. Now look. Nothing."

"The hot dog part was good," Maglioni said after taking a bite of the macaroni. "This has no flavor. It tastes like nothing."

Gilbert stared at his tapioca pudding. Perched atop his dessert, like a cherry on a sundae, was a small, grayish cylinder. "Holy cow, fellas," he said. "Look at this. *What* is this?"

Each of the boys peered at Gilbert's pudding, trying to identify the distasteful looking intruder.

"Maybe it's supposed to be there," Maglioni said. "Maybe it's part of the recipe."

"You got holes in your head, Maglioni?" Hazelnut said. "Even *this* place wouldn't put *that* thing in a pudding recipe."

"I know what it is!" Billy said. "Look at it. It's ash from Smitty's cigarette."

"Holy cow, it is," Gilbert said. "I can't eat this!"

"Tell the table officer," Maglioni said. "He'll let you get a new one."

"Yeah," Billy said. "Tell him. We'll go with you."

The four boys left their seats and approached Sergeant Major Sterelczyk, who was seated at the end of the long table. Gilbert showed him his pudding. "Uh, Sergeant, I have a problem with my pudding, sir. If you look closely, you'll see that some of Smitty's ash from his cigarette fell on my tapioca. I was wondering, sir, if I could take leave from eating my pudding today."

"Eat it," the sergeant major said in a calm and unconcerned manner.

"But, sir, you see that . . ."

"I said eat it, Corporal. That's an order. Eat it right here and now. Eat it in front of me before you return to your seat."

"Hey, that's not fair, Sergeant," Billy said. "He shouldn't be forced to eat Smitty's cigarette ash. It wasn't his fault."

The sergeant major remained calm. "Private . . . What's your name?"

"Roarke, sir."

"Private Roarke, you've just earned yourself a week of K.P. duty. One more word and I'll double it. Eat the pudding, Corporal. *All* of it."

Gilbert scooped a spoonful of pudding and ash, closed his eyes tightly and squeezed his nose with his left thumb and index finger as Maglioni held the tray for him. Gilbert stuck the spoon in his mouth as if it held a small pool of awful tasting cough medicine. He felt the ash dissolve into the pudding as it smashed against the roof of his mouth. He swallowed the unholy mixture as quickly as he could. A look of disgust covered his and his friends' faces.

Sergeant Major Sterelczyk was unmoved. "Cadets, return to your seats. Private Roarke, report to the kitchen today after class."

"What do I do there, sir?"

"You'll find out. Dismissed, Private."

Billy saluted the sergeant major. "Yes, sir."

Leonard was rinsing potatoes in the sink when Billy entered the kitchen and approached him. "Uh, Mr. Leonard? I'm here for K.P. duty. I'm Private Roarke."

"Mr. Leonard? Ain't nobody 'round here call me Mr. Leonard."

"Sorry, sir. What's your last name, sir?"

"Ain't nobody 'round here call me sir, neither. My last name is Jones. But you can call me Mr. Leonard. I like that one."

"Yes, sir."

Mr. Leonard turned off the water, dried his hands on his apron and turned toward Billy. "Now, what should I be callin' you?"

"Well, nobody around here calls me Billy. You can call me Billy if you'd like, sir."

Mr. Leonard put his hands on his hips and studied the young cadet. "Where'd you get your manners, boy?"

"From my parents, sir."

"Yeah, I guess that's where it happens. So, I gots me a helper, huh?"

"Yes, sir."

Mr. Leonard motioned with his arm for Billy to follow him. "All right, grab that peelin' knife, turn that bucket over, come here and sit down, and help Mr. Leonard peel some potatoes."

"Yes, sir. What are we making?"

Mr. Leonard laughed. "You funny, boy. We is makin' some hash. Gots to use that leftover meat somehow, and hash is 'bout the best way to make it so folks can get it down."

Billy and Mr. Leonard sat facing each other, peeling potatoes and allowing the skins to fall onto newspaper spread on the floor between them.

"No, boy, you gonna kill yourself that way. You'se peelin' the wrong way. Watch Mr. Leonard." He showed Billy the proper way to handle the peeling knife and remove the skin.

"Thanks. I think I got it now." Billy demonstrated a few swipes with the knife.

"Yeah, that's good. You learn good, boy."

"Thanks. Do you like cooking, Mr. Leonard?"

"I sure do, but what I do 'round here ain't cookin'."

"What do you mean?"

"Makin' food fo' two hundred boys ain't cookin', that's feedin'. No different than the barn. Just open it up and pour the slops in the trough. Now, my hash ain't bad. I'm able to do some creativity there. I add some secret ingredient and make it so it tastes pretty good. And I use real potatoes, so that's good."

"I haven't had your hash yet."

"Well, you in fo' a treat."

Billy set his first peeled potato in a big pot that already held several of Mr. Leonard's finished products. "What's your life's dream, Mr. Leonard?"

He gave Billy a bemused look. "Boy, you sure are a different breed o' cat. Where you get such talk 'bout my life's dream?"

"I remember standing in the mess line when someone complained about the food, and you said it wasn't your life's dream to be serving him his supper, or something like that."

"Hmm. My life's dream." He thought awhile before continuing. "Well, right now my dream is fo' my boy to come home safe. He's in trainin' with the 92nd Infantry in Arizona. He's a good boy. He's polite like you. Loves his mama and daddy. A good boy."

"What's his name?"

"His name's Earl. He's twenty-three. College graduate. First in my family."

"What college did he go to?"

"Small colored college in Alabama. He studied to make himself a lawyer. Wants to go to law school after the war."

"So you're from Alabama?"

"No, I's from Memphis."

"Memphis, Tennessee." Billy placed another peeled potato in the pot. "When did you move here?"

"My wife and I – all my children are growed up – moved here 'bout a year ago."

"Do you like it here?"

"Yeah. The weather's real nice. It get sticky in Memphis in the summer."

"Do you like the people here?"

"Oh, folks is folks. Same everwhere. Some good ones, some bad ones everwhere ya go."

Billy nodded. "I've lived in Pasadena all my life. I like it. Of course, I've never lived anywhere else. I like going other places, though. Sometimes, on Saturdays, I go to my mother's factory in Los Angeles. I like walking around there, just because it's different."

"Yeah."

"My dad's in the war, too. That's my dream, Mr. Leonard. For my dad to come home."

Mr. Leonard stopped his work and looked at Billy. "Well, let's hope 'n' pray it's the Lord's will fo' both of them to come home."

Billy stopped peeling and wiped his wet and tired hands on his pants. "So, do you think the war'll end soon?"

"I don't know 'bout that one. That Hitler's one mean human bein'. It's hard fo' me to imagine the great 'n' glorious Lord God Almighty creatin' that one. I think he sprung straight from hell, myself. But we's gonna beat 'im. I don't doubt that one. We's gonna do it."

"I wish we could just go in there and kill him."

Mr. Leonard shook his head as he spoke. "Well, it don't seem to work that way. Seems ya always gots to kill a whole mess o' decent folk justa get the one ya want. I know this ain't the Lord's way o' doin' things, I tell you that. This is people's way."

"You don't think we should be fighting the war?"

"No, I do. I'd be there myself if I could. I know things be a whole lot worse if Hitler be in charge over here. And I think things will be better fo' colored folk after this is over, seein' how our boys are over there fightin' 'n' dyin' like everone else." Mr. Leonard set the last potato in the pot and said, "I just don't think Jesus is smilin' right now."

CHAPTER

Sixteen

The Colonel stood in front of the room and struck his cane on Billy's desk. "Cadets, prepare for review of the state capitals. Private Hazelnut, Kentucky."

Hazelnut stood at attention. "Frankenfort, sir."

"Private Hazelnut, please try not to live down to your idiotic name. The capital of Kentucky is Frankfort, not Frankenfort."

"Yes, sir." Hazelnut sat down.

"Hillier, Arkansas."

Hillier rose, clicked his heels and stood at a firm attention. "Little Rock, sir."

"Corporal Hillier, we are not the Prussian cavalry. Please refrain from clicking your heels while stationed in my classroom."

"Yes, sir," Corporal Hillier replied as he clicked his heels and sat down.

"Longcoy, Pennsylvania."

Longcoy stood at attention, but did not answer.

"Let's move, Private. Your hesitation is wasting precious moments."

"Uh, Philadelphia, sir."

"Private Longcoy, explain the process which led you to state that Philadelphia is the capital of Pennsylvania."

"The process, sir?"

"Yes, Longcoy, the process."

"Well, sir . . . I soon realized that I didn't know the capital of Pennsylvania, so then I tried to think of the biggest city in Pennsylvania, and I thought of Philadelphia. And then I thought . . . well, Philadelphia is . . . that Philadelphia has a lot of history to it, so I came up with Philadelphia, sir."

"Congratulations, Longcoy, you are learning to think. I will inform the color guard. The school will undoubtedly want to honor you with a medal."

"Thank you, sir." Longcoy sat down.

"Unfortunately, all that your impressive brain has brought you is a wrong answer."

Longcoy stood. "Yes, sir."

"Harrisburg is the capital of Pennsylvania. All the history and glory and brotherly love of Philadelphia could not bring it to the status of state capital. Remember that, Longcoy. It's better to be right than smart."

"Yes, sir."

"Sit down. Gilbert, Vermont."

Gilbert stood at attention. "Montpelier, sir."

"Corporal Gilbert, do you speak French?"

"Yes, sir, I do."

"Don't speak it in this class."

"Yes, sir."

"Corporal Gilbert, is there anything you don't know?"

"Yes, sir. There are lots of things I don't know, sir."

The Colonel protruded his lips and nodded his head slowly. "You're a smart man, Corporal Gilbert."

"Thank you, sir."

"Start learning all those things you don't know."

"Yes, sir." Gilbert sat down.

"Private Roarke, Arizona."

Billy stood and answered, "Phoenix, sir."

"Why the godforsaken land of Arizona requires a state capital is beyond me. Don't you agree, Private Roarke?"

"Uhm, no, sir. I don't agree . . . sir."

"You don't? Explain, Private."

"Well, sir, I think there are a lot of great things about Arizona. There's the Grand Canyon and the Painted Desert and . . ."

"Private Roarke," the Colonel interrupted, "as soon as you enter this classroom tomorrow morning I want you to lay on my desk a one-page essay explaining, with your usual gifts, why in the name of God, natural landmarks such as the Grand Canyon and the Painted Desert require governance."

"Yes, sir."

"And don't begin to tell me that Gila monsters and jack rabbits should get the vote."

Several students wanted to laugh at this, but didn't.

"Yes, sir." Billy sat down.

"Cadets," the Colonel ordered, "take out your writing books and list from memory the capitals in alphabetical order. Corporal Gilbert, you are excused from this exercise. You are to read a book. And Private Roarke, you may begin your essay. You will need all the time you can muster, along with the wisdom of Solomon, to write an essay which will convert me to your idiotic thesis."

Roberts opened the latrine door and popped his dripping head through the opening. "Hey, somebody," he shouted, "gimme a towel!"

Billy was on his bunk, lying on his stomach writing, while Gilbert was polishing his shoes.

"Here ya go, Rob," Gilbert said as he tossed his polish rag to Roberts.

"Very funny, Gilbert. You're a real wise guy. I'm gonna take care o' you someday."

"That's sweet."

"I'm tossin' your rag in the toilet, Gilbert. Hey, Roarke, gimme a towel."

Billy sighed, then got a towel from his foot locker and threw it to Roberts.

Roberts wrapped the towel around his waist, walked to Billy's bunk and shook his head like a wet dog. "Hey, what're ya doin'?" he asked Billy.

"You got my paper wet. You wanna rewrite this for me?"

"No. What is it?" Roberts picked up the paper with wet hands.

"It's my homework."

"Homework?" Roberts read the paper. "I believe Arizona is worthy of a state capital because even though much of the land is a . . . What's that word? You got water on that word."

"No, *you* got water on that word. The word was barren."

Roberts continued reading. "Even though much of the land is a barren wasteland, there are inhabitants who need laws and governing." He looked up. "This is *stupid!*"

"I know it's stupid, but it's my assignment. I have to do it."

"That's *stupid!*"

Gilbert was now lying on his back with hands under his head. "Hey, Rob, the Colonel gave Roarke here this special assignment. Give the guy a break. Besides, didn't you have some trouble earlier this year with your teacher?"

"Yeah, what of it?"

"Well, my gentle sir, you should then appreciate Roarke's predicament. Feel pity for he who is walking where you once walked."

"Where are you from, Gilbert?"

Billy reached for his paper. "Can I have it back, please? Now I have to rewrite it."

"Here." Roberts handed the wet paper to Billy. "You shouldn't let teachers boss ya around like that. I never do."

"Is that a fact?" Gilbert said. "That wasn't you earlier this year, marching alone in the rain with a dunce cap on your head, singing at the top of your lungs 'God Bless America?' Or maybe you wanted to do that?"

"You got a lot o' guts, Gilbert, talkin' to me like that."

"All right, c'mon," Billy said. "Roberts, you can keep the towel."

"Yeah," Roberts said as he walked away.

"Gilbert," Billy said, "aren't you afraid to talk to him like that?"

"No. He'd never do anything to me."

"How do you know?"

"Because he knows I'm not afraid of him. He could clobber me but good, but he won't."

"Why not?"

"Some people, Roarke, only attack when they sense weakness and fear. Some dogs are like that, too. They won't bark unless they think you're afraid of them. Roberts knows I'm not afraid of him, so he doesn't clobber me."

"You're brave, Gilbert."

"I'm not brave. His kind just makes me mad. And when I'm mad, I'm not scared."

Billy nodded.

"You see, Roarke, Roberts is like Hitler."

"Hitler? He's not *that* bad."

"I know, I know. Just hear me out. Listen, it's easy for Hitler to send his tanks runnin' over Polish farmhouses, right? But just wait and see what he does once our G.I.s get close to him. My guess is he'll run like a scared rabbit. Mark my word; he won't be a man about it. He's strong on the outside and weak on the inside. And to a different degree, so is our good friend Roberts."

The next afternoon, Billy left his good friends on the junior school playground to retrieve a ball that was thrown over his head. The ball was lodged under a chain link fence, and as he lifted the web of slender metal he saw that it was loose and created a large opening. Large enough for someone to crawl through.

Several minutes later, he returned to the unsecured portion of the fence. He looked around and saw no one looking in his direction. He lifted the fence, lay down and crawled under. He got up quickly, looked back through the fence, again saw no one looking at him and quickly stepped backwards behind some bushes. Billy now stood alone on the sidewalk, unseen by anyone in school. He felt exhilarated. He felt brave. His heart was hammering his chest and he was happy. He started walking down the street, away from the school entrance.

He saw a car coming toward him and realized it might be someone from school. He looked straight ahead and tried to look relaxed, but all that trying made him look stiff and unnatural. The car drove on past the school. Billy kept walking.

CHAPTER

Seventeen

"Hey, where's Roarke?" Maglioni asked as he played catch with Gilbert and Hazelnut. "I haven't seen him for a long time."

"He must be in the can or on sick call," Hazelnut said. "Remember what we had for lunch?"

"Here he comes," Gilbert said as Billy approached them. "Hey, Roarke, where have you been? You sick?"

"No, I'm fine. Come over here, fellas."

He led the boys to a large oak tree. "Gather around me." The boys circled Billy, shielding him from the rest of the playground. "Get . . . a load . . . of this!" he said as he pulled a jar of pickles from his jacket pocket.

"Holy smokes, Roarke!" Gilbert said. "Where'd you get that?"

"At the market down the street."

"What?" the boys cried.

"How'd you get there?" Hazelnut asked.

"Under the fence."

"Roarke, not a keen idea," Gilbert said.

"And look at this." Billy pulled a wedge of Swiss cheese from his other pocket.

"How'd you pay for that?" Maglioni asked.

"I have some money, and I didn't need ration stamps for the cheese because it was old and the man was about to throw it out. He said I could come back next time for some old salami."

"Holy cow, Roarke," Gilbert said. "I can't believe you did this. Don't you know what they'd do to you if they caught you?"

"Yes, I do. They'd make me work with Mr. Leonard. And I actually enjoy that."

"Are you going to eat all that by yourself?" Hazelnut asked.

"Of course not. What kind of guy doesn't share with his pals? Fellas, we're eatin' good tonight."

When Billy came home the next weekend he found two letters from Sam and Andy. They had written before and Billy had responded with letters that explained all about military school, save for why he was there.

Sam's letter was covered with the black lines of the military censors, who made sure letter writers didn't reveal sensitive information, like the locations and movements of troops.

Andy's letters, like those from his father, had few black lines. Andy asked a lot of questions about military school and wondered how Billy's baseball career was coming along.

Billy had a good weekend. He went to work with his mother on Saturday, and together they had dinner in Chinatown. On Sunday afternoon he built a tree house with Charlie and Randall. It was also the first weekend home that he spent some time reading about the war.

Ever since the fight with Thomas, Billy had stopped his incessant monitoring of the war. Though he had access to newspapers at Eagleton, he rarely looked at them. His realization, formed at the witnessing of the G.I. shower, that he hated the war had remained and resulted in his trying to ignore it. He understood that knowing every detail about battles and developments would do nothing to return his father to him. The bad news just made him more anxious, and the good news gave him false hope.

But by this time Billy began engaging himself a bit more in the news of the war. He did not become immersed in its flood of information as before, but no longer did he ignore it. As knowledge would not bring his father back sooner, he also understood that neither would ignorance.

After Sunday dinner, before he returned to school, he sat at the dining room table and wrote a letter to his father. Then he wrote letters to Sam and Andy. He answered all their questions and asked them about their situations. He even drew and colored a map of Eagleton for each of them.

It was the last time he wrote the young men. He would never hear from them again.

The next evening, Maglioni and Hazelnut joined Billy and Gilbert at their bunks after dinner.

"Hey, Gilbert," Maglioni said, "remember how you once told me that if I wanted to dream about food I should just concentrate really hard on what I wanted to eat right before I went to sleep?"

"Yes."

"I tried your technique last night. I wanted to dream about a big chocolate cake and I didn't. Your technique doesn't work."

"What did you dream about?"

"I had a dream about a lemon cake with white frosting."

"They're in the same family, Maglioni," Hazelnut said. "You still had a dream about the cake family."

"Did you get to eat the lemon cake?" Gilbert asked.

"Yeah, I had a bite. It was good."

"Well, what are you complaining about? I helped you have a pretty good dream about a lemon cake. If it wasn't for me, you would've dreamt about the Colonel or something."

"I had a dream about the Colonel the other night," Billy said. "I dreamt I was seventy-five years old and I still had to turn in my daily essay on Arizona. I tried to have a dream about pot roast, but I don't think I had the proper concentration."

"Why are you still writing that essay?" Hazelnut asked.

Billy sighed. "The Colonel says I either write the essay every night until I convince him that Arizona deserves a state capital, or I admit to him that it doesn't."

"Why don't you give up, Roarke?" Hazelnut said. "You know the Colonel's never gonna give in. You'll be writing that stupid essay the rest of the year."

"Because, 'Nut," Gilbert said, "Roarke here has something you wouldn't understand. Roarke has convictions."

"I understand convictions, Gilbert, and I understand stupid. And this is a stupid waste of time. It's not like Roarke is standin' up for America or somethin'. He's standin' up for Arizona. Just say, 'Okay, boss, you win. Arizona doesn't deserve a state capital.' Besides, maybe the Colonel's right. Maybe Phoenix is a waste of time."

"That's not the point, 'Nut."

"Sure, *Bert*. Roarke is standing up for what he believes is right. I get that. It's just that his cause is so stupid."

"I admire Roarke," Maglioni said.

"Oooh, congratulations, Roarkey. You've got Maglioni on your side."

"Shut up, Hazelnut!" Maglioni shouted. He stood from his spot on Gilbert's bunk and pushed Hazelnut back a step.

Hazelnut stepped forward, grabbed Maglioni's tie and said, "Watch it, you little wop. I'll break you in two."

Billy stepped between the boys and separated them. "Okay, c'mon, fellas," he said, "break it up."

Maglioni was ready to cry. "Tell him to always stop making fun of me!"

"You attacked me, you stupid Italian squirt!"

"Hey, c'mon," Billy said. "Hazelnut, will you stop picking on Maglioni? He's supposed to be your friend."

"He pushed me. I didn't touch him."

"Just break it up." Billy put his arm on Maglioni's shoulder. "Mags," he said, "I know you got mad, but it's no good to start a fight."

"I know. I'm just tired of him always making fun of me."

"He's right, 'Nut," Gilbert said. "You're awful tough on the guy. Mags is okay."

"Yeah . . . well tell him not to push me anymore."

"C'mon, fellas," Billy said, "make up."

Maglioni stood and extended his hand. "Sorry I pushed you."

Hazelnut shook his hand. "Yeah, okay. Sorry I make fun of you sometimes. Pals?"

"Pals."

"Come to my bunk, Mags," Hazelnut said. "I'll show you this new Captain Midnight comic book I got last weekend."

"Well done, Roarke," Gilbert said when the two of them were left alone.

"Thanks."

"I always get nervous when guys are fighting. I don't know how to stop it."

"I don't know." Billy shrugged. "I guess you just separate them before it goes too far."

"Yeah. It never seems to go too far, though. Fellas seem to know when to stop. They let off a little steam, then they get scared and just kind of stop on their own. That's what I've observed."

"Yeah," Billy said, too quietly for Gilbert to hear.

CHAPTER

Eighteen

In April, Eagleton's football coach, Buzz Riley, started working with the junior school during their recess. This Monday afternoon he had the seventh graders with him on the athletic field.

Coach Riley was a middle-aged man dressed in a gray sweatshirt and baseball cap. A whistle hung from his neck and rested on his belly. "Huddle up, boys," he ordered. "On the double."

The boys gathered around him.

"All right, everybody, listen up. Next year you guys will be eligible for Eagleton sporting teams. We have a fine reputation for sporting excellence at Eagleton, and I will see that it continues. Football practice starts first thing next school year, so the sooner we start the better.

"The basic foundation of football is blocking and tackling. Today we'll learn to block. The pretty boys can't score the touchdowns unless the ugly mugs on the line do their jobs."

Coach Riley left the circle of boys that surrounded him. "All right, watch me. This is the lineman's stance." The coach crouched down and set his right arm straight to the ground, while his left forearm rested on his left leg. He lifted his head and strained to speak. "From this position you move forward and push your opponent back." Coach Riley lunged upward with middle-aged slowness. His face was red.

"Now, give me two straight lines facing each other, arms distance apart, and square off against an opponent on the opposite line. Let's go. On the double."

He blew his whistle and watched the boys arrange themselves as ordered. Billy was lined up against Maglioni.

"Now," he continued, "when I blow my whistle get in the lineman's stance. When I blow again, attack your opponent." The coach blew the signal and watched the boys drop down in a clumsy, uneven manner. He blew again and watched them greet each other with mild pushes.

"No. We're not dancing, boys. Keep your shoulders low and push. Push, men, push!"

They tried it again. "No. Heads up. Move your legs, boys! Move your legs. Let's go!"

Coach Riley had the boys continue the drill over and over. At the end of the line he stood over Billy.

"Sheez. What's your name, son?"

"Roarke, sir."

"I've seen you play, Roarke. I thought you were athletic. Push that kid. Hit him hard. Let's go."

Billy and Maglioni got in their lineman's stance. When the whistle blew, Billy lunged forward and pushed Maglioni with his shoulder.

"Roarke, hit that kid. Hard! That's an order."

"I'm trying, Coach."

"You look like a sissy, Roarke. Knock that kid on his can. He's half your size. Let's go!"

Riley blew his whistle and the boys again engaged. "That's it," he said. "Leave the field, Roarke. Get out of here."

"Where should I go, Coach?"

"I don't care. Go back to the barracks and get your beauty sleep."

"Yes, Coach."

Billy left the field, went to the empty barracks and lay on his bunk. About five minutes later, Gilbert came in. "I got kicked out, too, Roarke. Riley said you and I should take dancing lessons together."

"Swell."

"Hey, partner, want to join me in the auditorium? I haven't practiced my piano lesson in a while."

The auditorium was dark until Gilbert switched on the lights and walked with Billy to the piano on the stage. He placed his music on the stand and sat on the piano's bench.

Billy brought a chair from the auditorium floor and sat on the stage. He looked at the sheet music – Mozart's Sonata in C – as Gilbert began to play, even though Billy could not read the notes.

He thought his friend played very well, but Gilbert was enveloped in the frustration that comes only to those who know enough to be displeased. Billy heard music being played without mistakes. Gilbert heard himself maul Mozart with heavy fingers that pounded rather than kissed the keys.

"Gee, you're good, Gilbert."

"You're a pal, Roarke, but frankly I stink," he said without missing a note.

"It sounds good to me."

"I've had piano lessons since I was four. A chimpanzee could play this well with that much training. I've got no touch."

"Aw, you're being modest."

Gilbert shook his head. He finished the piece, then returned the sheet music to the beginning and started again. "You know, Roarke," he said, "I think it's going to happen pretty darn soon."

"What is?"

"D-Day. The invasion of France."

He looked at Gilbert. "Oh, yeah? What makes you think that?"

"It's been a long time – holy cow, I hate these broken octave chords – you know, the Allies have been training in England a long time. And I read an article recently that said the Allies have picked the date for the invasion. It's coming soon, I'm telling you. Mark my word."

"It shouldn't be that hard to invade France. I mean they'll bomb them a lot first, and the Germans are spread out all over – Russia, Italy. I mean they should make it okay, don't you think?"

Gilbert continued playing. "Oh, I'm sure, Roarke. You know, I think that's the first time I've heard you talk about the war. Say, your father's in England, right?"

"Yes, he's in the 101st Airborne – paratroopers."

"Paratroopers. Boy, he volunteered for that, didn't he? Your dad's a brave man, Roarke."

"Yeah."

"You must be proud."

"I am, Gilbert. I'm really proud."

After Gilbert finished playing, the boys returned to a full barracks. The cadets were relaxing before dinner. Some napped, others read, played cards or polished brass.

Outside, Cadet Maglioni was running down the hall. He had news. Big news.

CHAPTER

Nineteen

Maglioni burst through the barracks door like a full-back. "Fellas! Fellas!" he shouted. "You won't believe it!"

"Pipe down, you little wop," Roberts said as he rose sleepily from his bunk.

"What is it, Mags?" Gilbert asked.

"Everyone who has the Colonel, come over here." Maglioni walked swiftly as about eight cadets followed him to his bunk.

"What's the idea?" Hazelnut said. "This better be good."

"It's better than good." Maglioni beamed. "Fellas, what would you wish for more than anything else in the world?"

"A steak," Longcoy said.

"No, no. Besides food."

"Get to the point," Hazelnut said.

"Wait a minute," Billy said. "Does this have something to do with the Colonel? You said . . ."

"Yes!" Maglioni beamed brighter than before.

"Tell us! What? C'mon, Mags!" The boys demanded the news, and now other cadets began to crowd around.

"Okay, okay, fellas." Maglioni quieted the crowd. "Listen to this. I just found out that the commandant has *fired* the Colonel. Today was his last day!"

The group erupted again. "What? No foolin'? Don't kid around like that, Maglioni."

"I'm not foolin', fellas."

"How do you know this, Mags?" Gilbert asked.

"Lieutenant Mitchell just told me. Outside the commandant's office. He was in there when Major Chandler was telling someone he fired him. He said his performance was 'disgraceful'."

"This better be on the level," Hazelnut said.

"It is! It is! Be happy! It is! Look, there's the lieutenant. Ask *him*!"

Lieutenant Mitchell entered the barracks and walked over to the cadets.

"Is it true, Lieutenant?" Gilbert asked. "Did Chandler really give the Colonel the heave-ho?"

"Yes, Corporal. *Major* Chandler did give him the heave-ho. I was in his office and heard it all. He fired your teacher. He won't be back tomorrow."

"Yippee! Hooray!" The cadets shouted their happiness.

"You guys act like the war ended," Mitchell said.

"It has ended for us," Hazelnut replied. "No jap or kraut ever did me in like the Colonel. He's been my only enemy this year, Lieutenant."

"Hey," Billy said, "no more Arizona essays. I'm done! Yippee!"

The boys jumped up and down, slapping each other on the back, celebrating like they'd won the World Series. Maglioni and Metz even danced with each other. Their barracks leader smiled faintly and walked to his quarters.

Roberts stood from his nearby bunk. "You little girls are the biggest bunch of saps I've ever seen."

"What's it to you, Roberts?" Hazelnut said. "Let us enjoy ourselves. This is *our* celebration."

"Sure, you boys and girls continue your little party. Just think about one thing. Maybe they fired your Colonel, but what makes you think they're gonna hire Shirley Temple to be your teacher? I've got news for you children. There's worse out there than the Colonel, and you just might be getting it."

The cadets ignored Roberts's warning. "Aw, can it, Rob," Hazelnut said. "You're not going to spoil our fun. We've *had it* with the Colonel. We'll take *anybody* over him. This is the best day of my life!"

The boys continued to shout and dance and laugh. Nothing, not even Roberts, could end their joy.

The seventh grade cadets woke the next morning like they never had before. The fast slaps of feet on the floor replaced their usual groans and moans upon hearing reveille. They were polite in the latrine, wishing each other good morning while waiting patiently for sinks and toilets.

They cleaned the barracks with a vigor usually saved for playtime. Last night they didn't complain about dinner, and this morning they thought breakfast was delicious. During drill they seemed to bounce. Marching that morning was, for the first time, not tedium, but a chance to breathe crisp, cool air and to feel the warmth of the new sun. Happiness gave them energy and made everything cleaner, brighter, better.

"Boy," Hazelnut said in the barracks before class, "this is a day I'm going to mark on my calendar and celebrate every year – April 18, 1944."

"Hey, fellas," Billy said, "we should get together on this date, wherever we are, for the rest of our lives. The whole class."

"Swell idea, Roarke. A reunion. Count me in," Gilbert said.

"I wonder what our new teacher will be like," Maglioni said.

"I don't care. It doesn't matter to me," Hazelnut replied. "Just so long as it's not the Colonel."

Maglioni smiled. "I hope he's nice."

"He'll be nice," Billy said. "I have a feeling things are looking up for us."

"I agree, Roarke," Gilbert said. "And it's high time."

The seventh grade marched with great anticipation to their classroom. They were still happy, but now a bit of anxiety entered their minds. Who would their new teacher be? And what would he be like?

Hazelnut was the first cadet to enter the classroom, and the look on his face spread like dominoes falling to each boy in line.

He stood in front of the chalkboard writing arithmetic problems. When finished, he turned, took two steps and set his cane to the floor. The Colonel stood before them.

The class seated themselves, stunned. After the Pledge, the Colonel addressed the cadets.

"I am fully aware of the fact that a large portion of the energy you expend is devoted to the manly art of gossip and storytelling. That no bit of information, large or small, true or false, ever rests in the mind of one of you, but travels from mouth to mouth like a plague, until the whole of you is infected. Since I am certain that you have already invested a great deal of chatter concerning this matter, I risk repeating what you already know."

The students brightened, thinking that the Colonel sounded like he was announcing his departure and that *this* would be his last day.

"I must, however, make it official. Mr. Tredwiller is no longer your study hall teacher."

The mad joy the boys had felt was now completely demolished. The news of the Colonel's firing had given them a happiness that reached so high that the opposite truth gave them a sadness that fell so low, fulfilling a law of emotional symmetry. Nothing had changed concerning the Colonel. He was their teacher yesterday, and he was their teacher today. But today that fact was devastating.

Their disappointment was so strong there was no way of camouflaging the look it brought to their faces. The Colonel misinterpreted the look.

"At ease. You will be protected from yourselves. The commandant has arranged for another zoo keeper, who, I believe, will begin this evening. Begin the arithmetic exercise."

"Nice work, Maglioni," Hazelnut said while standing in the lunch line. The Colonel's fired, huh? You got the wrong teacher."

"I didn't get anything wrong. Lieutenant Mitchell told me it was the Colonel. He never said it was Mr. Tredwiller."

"Lay off him, Hazelnut," Billy said. "It's not his fault."

"But I'm mad."

"We're all mad," Billy replied.

"I'm sorry, fellas," Maglioni said.

"No need to apologize, Mags," Gilbert said.

Soon after the boys sat down to a lunch of biscuits and gravy, Roberts joined them across the table.

"So, girls, how was your *new* teacher today?"

"Shut up, Roberts!" Hazelnut cried.

The table officer, Lieutenant Miller, looked up from his tray. "Hey, clam up down there."

Hazelnut lowered his voice, but kept his tone. "Don't say another word, Roberts. I'm warning you. Not now. *Don't say another word.*"

Roberts smirked. "What's the little girl gonna do about it?"

What the little girl did about it was to stand up, lift his tray, and heave his biscuits and gravy onto Roberts's uniform.

Roberts sat there stunned. "Lieutenant!" he cried. "Look what he did!"

Before Roberts finished speaking, Lieutenant Miller grabbed Hazelnut by the arm and marched him toward the commandant's office.

Roberts surveyed the mess that dripped from his shirt like a slow-moving avalanche. "I'm gonna kill that guy. What am I gonna do?"

"How about a G.I. shower?" Billy said. "That would work."

"'Nut warned you, Rob," Gilbert said, "but you kept letting him have it."

"You guys are gonna pay." Roberts stood and turned to the officer at the table behind him. "Permission to change uniforms, sir."

"Permission granted, Corporal."

"Oh, not here, Rob," Gilbert said. "That would be in such poor taste."

"Shut up, Gilbert!" Roberts shouted and left the table.

"Oh, poor 'Nut," Gilbert said.

"What do you think they'll do to him?" Maglioni asked.

"No idea," Gilbert replied. "I've never seen anybody throw their lunch at someone. I imagine they'll treat this pretty seriously. Poor 'Nut."

Major Chandler spoke to Hazelnut and Roberts together in his office that afternoon. After listening to both boys, he first told Roberts that there must be no retaliation whatsoever. And if he did attempt anything against Cadet Hazelnut, he would be subject to severe consequences. After Roberts agreed, he was dismissed, and Hazelnut was left to receive his punishment.

The commandant gave Hazelnut thirty demerits, KP for a week, and promised a phone call to his parents. Hazelnut said he understood, at which point Major Chandler said he was also waiting for an apology. Hazelnut apologized.

CHAPTER

Twenty

M r. C.J. Kooler, a retired high school mathematics teacher who lived nearby, was the new study hall teacher. He was a short gentleman with a bow tie and glasses that he tilted downwards when speaking to someone.

He began his first night at Eagleton by rolling the teacher's chair to the front of the class and sitting in it. When the cadets were seated, he looked around the room and greeted each boy with a nod and a smile. The class sat silently, some smiling back, others looking bewildered.

"Good evening, boys," he said to them as if he were sitting in his parlor and pleased to have them visiting his home.

"Good evening, sir," most of the cadets replied.

"My name is Mr. Kooler, and I am your new study hall teacher. Let me tell you that it is a pleasure to be here – to be among such fine boys as yourselves."

The class looked around at each other, not quite sure how to respond to such a nice man.

"I know you have assignments to contend with, but before you begin your studies I ask that you allow me the indulgence of sharing with you some of the interesting things I read and learn during the day. The only good thing about retirement, boys, is the time it gives for reading. That, and the much improved state of my garden."

Mr. Kooler lifted a magazine from his lap and opened it. "Do you like cartoons, boys?"

"Yes, sir."

"There are none like those in *The New Yorker*. And I also love the splendid little gems from Mr. Brubaker's column. Allow me to read you one. Listen to this, boys:

> *'Experts have figured out that the war*
> *will cost well over a trillion dollars.*
> *If we could only agree not to have another*
> *war until this one has been paid for, we*
> *might really have peace in our time.'"*

The class responded with light laughter.

Mr. Kooler smiled and nodded. "What a pleasure it is to be here. I have so much to share with you, and so much I'd like to hear from you. And yet, you are here to study."

Billy raised his hand.

"Yes, young man."

He stood. "Mr. Kooler, sir, we don't have a lot of school-work to finish tonight. Just to let you know that you don't have to stop talking."

"Splendid. Oh, sit down, my boy. There's no need to stand in this class. You have had a long day and are tired. I am old and am tired. We will sit together."

He sat down. "Yes, sir."

"What is your name, my boy?"

"Roarke, sir."

"Roarke. Splendid. Roarke, tell me something about yourself. I want all of you to tell me something about yourselves. Perhaps one boy each evening. Do you mind, Roarke? Do you mind being the first?"

"No, sir. What do you want to know?"

"Tell me what you love. Tell me what you love more than anything in this world."

Billy thought.

"But that is not fair," Mr. Kooler said. "I must be first. If I am to lead this study hall, I must do first what I ask of you. I will go first, Roarke. I will tell you what I love."

Mr. Kooler took off his glasses, held them in his hands, and looked up. "I love music and mathematics. I love books and gardens." He looked at Billy. "Those are the things I love. What do you love, young Roarke? What stirs you deep inside?"

"My family, sir. I love my family the most. More than anything else."

Mr. Kooler saw Billy's moist eyes. "Forgive me, my boy. I have intruded."

Billy smiled. "That's okay, Mr. Kooler. If you want to know what else I love, it's mostly sports. Baseball and football."

"Ah, a sportsman. And I can tell by your face you are a scholar, as well. You read, don't you, young Roarke?"

"Yes, sir. I read a lot."

Mr. Kooler nodded. "The Greek ideal – body and mind – lives in you, young Roarke. And you must possess a marvelous character."

"No, sir. Not all the time."

Mr. Kooler gave Billy a puzzled look. "But of course not all the time. It is not possible for us, all the time. Were it our nature, our instinct, our unavoidable urge to commit goodness and right, it would be as constant with us as breathing." He waved his hand. "And there would be nothing else."

Billy looked at Mr. Kooler as he put his glasses in his coat pocket.

"That is why goodness should be celebrated," Mr. Kooler said as his head moved to change his focus from Billy to the entire class. "It is very difficult for us. Very difficult, indeed."

A Brahms symphony played on the radio as the students did their schoolwork. The classroom at night looked like a different place. A different light shone on its objects. And with Mr. Kooler as the teacher, it had indeed become a very different place.

CHAPTER

Twenty-one

The seventh grade gathered on the athletic field, awaiting instructions from Coach Riley. "All right, boys," he said, "today we're going to practice the forward pass. Get in . . . oh heck, my whistle. Ah heck. Roarke, hey, Roarke, run to my quarters will ya and grab my whistle. I think I left it on my bunk."

Billy ran to the staff quarters and knocked on the door. No one answered, so he entered as ordered. The room was much smaller than the barracks and the lone window had blinds, which were drawn. The lights were off and the room was dark, save for a line of light that shone from under the closed latrine door. Billy stood and waited for his eyes to adjust to the darkness. He started walking and inspecting the bunks, looking for Coach Riley's whistle. He found it. As he picked it up, his eyes met something resting on a nearby bed. *What's that?* he thought to himself. *What is that?* Billy walked closer to the object and saw what it was. His heart jumped as he uttered an involuntary, "Ah!"

Just then a spray of light hit Billy as the latrine door opened. The Colonel entered the room on crutches wearing nothing but a towel around his waist. The Colonel stopped when he saw Billy. He straightened his back and stared at the boy. All his weight now rested on his right leg. His only leg.

Billy looked again at the object on the bunk, the artificial leg, then turned to face his teacher. He wanted to say he was sorry. Sorry that he intruded on the Colonel's privacy, but most of all sorry that the Colonel had lost a leg. But Billy could not speak.

The Colonel broke the silence. "What are you doing here?"

"Uh . . . sorry, sir," he replied. "Coach, uhm . . . Coach Riley told me to get his whistle."

"Did you get it?"

"Yes, sir."

"Then get out."

"Yes, sir."

Billy walked back to the field and handed the whistle to Coach Riley. He was numb. He was the only cadet in the school who knew why the Colonel had been discharged from the army. The Colonel never slugged Patton, cursed Ike, or drove a tank through the White House. The Colonel had lost a leg. Billy knew it, and he wished to God that he didn't.

Billy entered class the next morning scared. Not just intimidated as usual, but scared. He thought the Colonel would be furious with him and would just let him have it with some kind of punishment that would make the Arizona essay seem like a privilege. He had thought of going on sick call, but decided not to.

He sat at his desk and avoided looking at the Colonel, who was seated behind his desk rather than in his usual position of standing in front of the class.

The Colonel stood and led the cadets in the Pledge of Allegiance, then immediately sat down again. Billy didn't think the Colonel's voice sounded particularly angry, so he took a quick look at him.

The Colonel did not look directly at Billy, but looked comfortably at the class as he addressed them. "This morning, cadets, you are to write an essay on the topic of 'courage.' You will have one hour. Are there questions?"

Few students ever asked questions of the Colonel, but Corporal Hillier, perhaps taking inspiration from the theme of the assignment, stood at attention, clicked his heels and asked, "Sir, do you want an essay which tells what courage is, or do you want us to give examples of courage?"

The Colonel rested his chin on a hand and replied, "You may decide, Hillier."

The class was surprised. The Colonel made no criticism concerning Hillier's question, no comment about him clicking his heels; the Colonel simply answered him. And the answer itself was cause for surprise. Corporal Hillier was allowed to make a decision, albeit a small one. The Colonel had made all the decisions in class, large and small. All of them, until now.

"Any further questions? Begin."

Billy looked at his teacher while pulling his writing book from his desk. The Colonel opened a newspaper, laid it flat on his desk and read.

Billy wrote a story about his dad. It was something his mother had told him. When his father was in junior high school there was a boy who was teased by his schoolmates.

The boy was big and clumsy, and not a good student. One time during lunch, as he sat alone, a table of boys started throwing food at him. Sometimes food would hit him in the face or land on his lunch, but he pretended not to notice. When Billy's father saw this he picked up his lunch, left his own friends and sat next to the boy. The food-throwing stopped.

After Billy finished writing he checked the story for mistakes, then pulled a book from his desk and read.

The Colonel remained seated after an hour had passed and now had the class read aloud their essays. When each cadet finished the Colonel had no remarks, bad or good, and simply called on the next student to read.

After Billy read his essay and seated himself, the Colonel rose from his desk and walked with his cane to the front of the room. He stood straight and moved his head slowly, looking each young boy in the eye. He saw that none of them looked at his legs. Finally, he looked at Billy. He remained standing as the rest of the cadets read their essays.

Before the period ended, the Colonel spoke. "You have an exam in history this afternoon. I strongly suggest you study during your lunch period. The rigor you pursue now will profit you later. That is maturity. Practice it. Class dismissed. Private Roarke, report to my desk."

Billy met the Colonel and stood before him as the man took his seat. "Yes, sir?"

The Colonel waited for the rest of the class to leave before speaking. "Private Roarke," he said in his usual tone, "please do not burden me any further with your Arizona essays. I am ordering you to cease this exercise."

"Yes, sir."

"Dismissed."

Billy left the class and ran to catch up with his friends to tell them the good news. They all congratulated him, patting him on the back and generally reacting as if he'd been promoted to sergeant.

"Hey, Roarke," Hazelnut said, "someday you should take a trip to Phoenix and send the Colonel a postcard of the state capitol building."

"Nope. I'm never going to think about Arizona again. And I'll sure never visit there. *No, sir.*"

In the mess hall Billy and his friends sat together over a lunch of chicken and dumplings.

"What's gotten into Leonard?" Hazelnut said. "This stuff is good."

"Mr. Leonard is a good cook," Billy said. "He just doesn't usually have good ingredients."

"Why don't you get him some next time you're at the market?" Hazelnut said.

"Shhh. Keep it quiet, 'Nut," Gilbert said. "That topic is hush-hush."

"Hey," Maglioni said, "what do you fellas think got into the Colonel this morning? He was different. Roarke, you talked to him alone. What do you think?"

"Gee, I don't know. I didn't notice anything."

"Are you kidding me?" Hazelnut said. "The whole class reads their essays and not once does he criticize anyone. That's strange."

"Maybe he's sick," Maglioni said.

"Yeah, maybe," Gilbert said. "But he must be *really* sick. Oslander reads his essay about the time he thought his dog was courageous because even though he knew he'd get in trouble for going to the bathroom in the house, he didn't run away. And then Oslander says, 'He took his punishment like a man.' Good grief. I thought the Colonel was going to anni-hilate him for that."

"The Colonel did get a strange look on his face," Hazelnut said, "when Oslander ended his essay with, 'So that's why I think dogs have more courage than people,' but he just sat there and said nothing."

"Oh," Gilbert said, "there's definitely something screwy going on with the old boy, especially since he freed Roarke here from the Arizona essays. Yep, something *real* screwy all right."

Throughout the week the Colonel continued to refrain from criticism of the cadets. Several rumors began to spread, which served to explain the strange behavior. The most pop-ular theory held that General Patton, who was from the Pasadena area, was coming home on leave and was "looking for the Colonel," and that the Colonel was afraid to fight him again. There were several other rumors which concerned Nazi spies, religious conversion and dating Betty Grable.

At the end of class on Friday, the Colonel asked for the cadets' attention before he spoke to them. "I have known for some time," he began, "that there is quite a bit of nonsense dispensed among you and others concerning me, most specif-ically the conditions surrounding my discharge from the army."

The cadets' eyes became alert as they adjusted themselves in their seats, preparing for exciting news.

"Not surprisingly," he continued, "one hundred percent of it is rubbish. Being that you are human beings, you certainly have no control over your condition and its subsequent folly. However, I will say, on some of your behalves, that, happily, this instinctual urge towards ignorance is not uniform. Some of you show greater sense than others.

"I will not recite the entire list of theories which have attached themselves to me, only to say, however, that I do regret that the tale concerning Miss Grable is false."

The class laughed for the first time all year.

"I will now tell you the truth of my discharge. I was a tank commander in North Africa. I served under General George S. Patton, and I can honestly say that I never laid hand nor glove on the man, though there were times it was considered."

The class laughed again and the Colonel paused before continuing. "During a battle in Tunisia I was wounded and sent to a field hospital. It was there that I had my left leg amputated. That is why I walk with a cane. And that is why I was discharged. Are there any questions?"

The class stared at the Colonel and said nothing.

"No questions?"

The class had none.

"Then you are dismissed."

The cadets slowly left their seats and walked to the door.

"Sir," Gilbert said to the Colonel as he rose from his desk, "thank you for your sacrifice."

The class stopped, turned and looked at their teacher. "Corporal Gilbert," the Colonel replied gently, "losing only one's leg in battle is not sacrifice. I hope you never truly understand that."

Gilbert didn't respond, and, with the rest of the class, slowly turned his head away from his teacher and left the room.

CHAPTER

Twenty-two

It was now the middle of May and in one month the school year would end. Billy would be home and the summer would be wonderful for what it didn't have. For three months he would be able to walk without marching, talk without standing, and eat without wincing. His days would not begin and end with a bugle, and his dreams could be filled with something other than food. His buckle could be rusty, and the shoes he'd wear would need no polish. The absence of things is what he wished for now.

But Billy was beginning to enjoy Eagleton. He had become used to the routines of the school. He could "Parade Rest" and "Right Flank March." He liked his friends, especially Gilbert, and no one really bothered him too much. The biggest change, though, was in the classroom. The Colonel remained stern and sober, but the harshness that appeared to leave him after Billy learned of his leg remained at large. The Colonel did not become an easy man, but no longer was he an intolerable one.

And Billy loved Mr. Kooler. Study hall had become his favorite time. It was the day's dessert.

So, as the entire corps of cadets began to prepare for Parents' Day, with its parade and inspections, Billy could honestly echo Gilbert when he said that Eagleton was really not so bad.

There were several major inspections during the school year, and though the one preceding Parents' Day was not the most important in terms of the military system, the administration considered it vital. They desperately wanted the parents to see Eagleton at its shiniest. Parents paid tuition.

Lieutenant Mitchell was particularly demanding during the few days before Friday's inspection. He ordered the cadets to polish the metal rails of their beds with their brass cleaner so they would shine like silver. He brought a ruler to each bunk and checked that the white sheet overlapping the blanket near the pillow would be exactly four inches. He even made the cadets lie on the floor under their beds and wipe each of the dozens of bed springs, small coils which wouldn't even be seen by inspectors.

On Friday morning Lieutenant Mitchell, as usual, supervised the effort, moving swiftly and sternly from one cadet to the next. "Private Priedler."

"Yes, sir?" Priedler stopped scrubbing and looked up from his seated position near a toilet.

"Do you like ice cream?"

"Yes, sir. Sure do, sir."

"You will be eating it off that toilet seat after inspection. Would you eat off it now, Private?"

"No, sir."

"Then it's not clean. Start scrubbing, Priedler." Lieutenant Mitchell found another cadet. "Maglioni, I see stained shower tiles. You will be served wop food on that shower floor you're pretending to wipe. I suggest you make it spic 'n' span."

"Yes, sir."

Lieutenant Mitchell then spoke generally to all the cadets working in the latrine. "All of you will be served food on the surface you are cleaning. Roarke, Gilbert, you will eat out of those sinks. Simpson, Bernier, you will eat off the floor. Do I make myself clear?"

They answered together, "Yes, sir."

"What did you say?"

"Yes, sir!"

The cadets scrubbed harder, pouring more cleanser on their assigned surfaces and rubbing as if to save their lives. Lieutenant Mitchell was pleased with himself. He smiled at the increased fervor in the latrine and left to similarly motivate the cadets working in the barracks.

The inspection would take place Friday afternoon and as the cadets awaited the arrival of the commandant and the BC, they made last-minute adjustments and a few more quick wipes of buckles and shoes.

"All right, Barracks C," Lieutenant Mitchell said, "put everything away and get ready. Make one last check of your uniform and living area. Remember, if we're the cleanest, it should make us a cinch for Honor Barracks." He turned to a cadet adjusting his pillow and said, "Lyle, tuck your shirt in. Move it, Lyle. For once in your life don't be a pig."

Billy took one last wipe of his shoes and buckle, and placed the rag back in his footlocker.

"All right, everybody," Mitchell said, "standby for inspection."

The cadets straightened footlockers, pillows and themselves one last time before standing at the head of their beds awaiting the inspectors.

After a few minutes the door opened and Lieutenant Mitchell ordered, "Barracks, atten . . . hut!"

The cadets stiffened like toy soldiers, staring straight and appearing not even to breathe.

The battalion commander, Tom Kirkendall, followed by two cadet officers, entered the barracks with eyes looking everywhere at once. Cadet Captain Kirkendall was a handsome seventeen-year-old boy who carried himself with the confidence and maturity of a highly accomplished man. He returned Mitchell's salute without looking at him. "Lieutenant."

The BC and his officers walked slowly around the barracks, inspecting each cadet and his area. "The commandant is indisposed," he said, "so it will just be us, Lieutenant."

"Yes, sir."

"We will provide a full report."

"Yes, sir."

Billy enjoyed hearing Lieutenant Mitchell say, "Yes, sir," to another cadet, but his face showed no satisfaction. He continued to stare straight ahead, putting forth great energy into doing nothing.

Captain Kirkendall stopped before Corporal Roberts's bunk and studied the large eighth grader from cap to shoes. He put a white glove on his right hand, squatted and swept his index finger on the floor beneath the bed. He stood and inspected his finger.

"This barracks is outstanding, Lieutenant," he said while looking at the corporal.

"Thank you, sir," Mitchell replied from his corner of the room.

The BC continued his tour, flipping dimes on beds, looking intently at many things and finding nothing wrong – no dust, no dirt, no imperfection. Just straight, clean lines of beds, cadets and gear. He walked past Gilbert and Billy, by now tired of studying cadets, and walked into the latrine with his staff.

Muffled voices were heard as the latrine was inspected, then laughter. Kirkendall and his staff returned serious and silent, as if back on stage and into roles that did not smile.

"Lieutenant Mitchell," Captain Kirkendall said, "do your cadets eat in that latrine?"

"No, sir."

"Well they could. Very impressive."

"Thank you, sir."

As the captain stood near the latrine door he looked lazily to his right before dropping his eyes to Billy's footlocker. "Private," the BC said.

"Yes, sir," Billy said with confidence.

"Your footlocker is unlatched."

"Yes, sir," Billy said without confidence.

Kirkendall and his staff walked over to Lieutenant Mitchell. This time the BC looked at the barracks leader. "Well done, Lieutenant."

"Thank you, sir."

"Generally speaking, your barracks sparkles. You and your cadets are to be commended."

"Thank you, sir."

"The commandant will be fully informed. As you were." The BC returned Lieutenant Mitchell's salute and left the barracks.

With the battalion staff gone the cadets seemed to breathe again, their stiff bodies loosening as they patted one another on the back and offered congratulations. An exhausted happiness filled the room.

"Lieutenant," Private Priedler said, "are you still going to make us eat off the toilets?"

Mitchell smiled. "No, Private. We passed with flying colors. Honor Barracks cadets don't eat in the latrine."

"Thank you, sir!"

Piercing through the relaxed and relieved atmosphere like a flaming arrow was Corporal Roberts, who took a direct path to Billy's bunk.

"You!" Roberts shouted as he found the boy sitting on his bed talking to Gilbert. "You're the only black mark we got! We had a perfect inspection except for you! We worked hard for two days getting this barracks perfect and you ruined it for us!"

"Knock it off, Roberts," the lieutenant said. "I'll deal with that myself."

Billy looked at Roberts calmly and said, "It was a mistake. Take it easy. The BC still thought we had a great barracks."

"Yeah, Rob," Gilbert said. "Go back to your cage."

"I'm sick of you and your friends, Gilbert!" Roberts pointed to Billy. "We worked to be *perfect*, and *he* ruined it for us!"

Gilbert stood. "By golly, Rob, you are truly a . . ."

Roberts interrupted Gilbert by reaching below Billy's bed and grabbing his footlocker. Billy stood to stop him, but Roberts pushed him away. He opened the locker and lifted it to his chest.

"Drop the locker, Roberts," Lieutenant Mitchell said. "That's an order."

He disobeyed him. Instead of dropping it, he turned his body and swung the locker with great force, holding onto the case as all its contents flew out. Towels, clothes, shoes, soap, a baseball, books . . . All of Billy's belongings at school flying and falling at distances determined by their size and weight.

Of all the things launched from the locker, one item stood out. Its arc through the air was higher and longer, and its landing more dramatic.

As the entire barracks watched, a jar of pickles, with its own flight pattern, crashed to the floor. Small pieces of glass shot outward in all directions, while whole cucumbers slid along the hardwood like sleds on snow. Immediately, the entire room smelled of vinegar.

All eyes turned from the floor to Billy, then to the door. Through which entered Cadet Captain Kirkendall.

CHAPTER

Twenty-three

Lieutenant Mitchell's voice was a mixture of command and concern. "Barracks, atten . . . hut."

"What is going on here?" the BC asked without returning the lieutenant's salute.

"Sir," Lieutenant Mitchell replied, "Corporal Roberts took it upon himself to empty the footlocker of Private Roarke, sir."

"And what is this, Lieutenant?" he asked as he walked to the crash site and pointed to the pickles.

"Sir, it is a broken jar of pickles."

"I can see that, Lieutenant. What is it doing in this barracks? Who is Private Roarke?"

"I am, sir." Billy raised his hand.

The BC walked to Billy, stood directly in front of the boy and stared at him for a moment before speaking. "Private."

"Yes, sir."

"I assume you are aware of the rule concerning bringing food from home."

"Yes, sir."

Gilbert, standing at attention, moved his head a little and looked at Billy with a face that was afraid for his friend.

"How did you sneak that past the guard?"

"I didn't, sir."

Captain Kirkendall brought his hands to his hips and spread his legs farther apart, his body revealing a seething impatience. "You didn't, Private? You deny bringing that on campus? What is your story, Private?"

"I didn't bring the food from home, sir." Billy's voice started to shake, but he didn't cry. "I left school and got it at the market down the street."

"What? You went AWOL? When, Private?"

"I've gone twice, sir. The last time was last week."

Captain Kirkendall turned swiftly to walk toward Lieutenant Mitchell. After a few steps, he stopped and turned to Roberts. "What did you know about this, Corporal?"

"Nothing, sir," Roberts said while standing at a strict attention, the empty locker at his feet.

"Then why did you empty the footlocker, Corporal?"

"I was mad about it being unlatched, sir. We worked hard to get this barracks perfect. We want Honor Barracks, sir. Roarke was our only black mark, sir."

The BC turned away from Roberts and approached Mitchell. "Were you aware, Lieutenant, that you had cadets going AWOL for pickles?"

"No, sir."

"What else is going on here, Lieutenant?"

"Nothing, sir."

An angry Captain Kirkendall stood before a stiff Lieutenant Mitchell. "How would you know, Lieutenant? It seems to me you don't know much of what goes on in Barracks C."

"Yes, sir."

"Do Honor Barracks cadets go AWOL for pickles, Lieutenant?"

"No, sir."

"*No, they don't.*"

"Sir . . ." the barracks leader began in a voice that sounded like he might begin to cry.

"I'm not ready to hear any more of this, Mitchell. The commandant, I'm sure, will be happy to take over from here."

"Yes, sir."

The BC pointed a finger at the barracks leader and said with teeth tightly together, "Get this barracks squared away, Lieutenant."

"Yes, sir."

"Get it squared away *now.*"

Captain Kirkendall returned Lieutenant Mitchell's salute with a swift chop and left the barracks, the acrid smell of vinegar still hanging in the air.

Billy lay in bed that night thinking about what might happen to him. If the commandant kicked him out of Eagleton for going AWOL, where would he go to school? At the time it didn't seem like he'd done anything real bad. He figured he'd get demerits and K.P. duty if he got caught. All he did was get some food at the market. He didn't hurt anyone. He didn't beat anyone. He didn't send anyone to the hospital.

But the reaction of Captain Kirkendall, a cadet officer Billy respected, made him think he'd done a very bad thing. He was not, however, worried about himself; he was worried about his mother. He would cause her grief one more time.

As he turned to his side to try and sleep, he felt a strong hand grab his blanket and the sheet that covered him, and rip them off his body. Billy looked up, startled, to see Lieutenant Mitchell standing over him.

"Get out of bed, Roarke."

"Yes, sir."

"Come here."

He followed Mitchell into the latrine. The floor was cold under Billy's bare feet and he squinted as the lieutenant turned on the bright lights.

"I still smell pickles, Roarke," Mitchell said as he stood close to Billy, his head tilted down at the younger boy. "Do you still smell pickles?"

"Yes, sir."

"You didn't do a good job cleaning up, did you, Roarke?"

"No, sir." Billy stood with his arms folded against his chest, protecting himself from the cold of the latrine and the heat of the lieutenant.

"How long do you think it will take to get the smell out of my barracks, Roarke?"

"I don't know, sir."

"I do." The lieutenant twice poked his finger in Billy's chest. "*All night.*"

"All night, sir?"

"You're not sleeping tonight, Roarke. I've got an all-night watch on you. You will be scrubbing that floor *all night.*"

"Yes, sir."

Lieutenant Mitchell left to fill a bucket with water. He brought the bucket, a can of cleanser and a stiff brush, and dropped them on the floor by Billy's feet. "You ruined our chances of getting Honor Barracks, Roarke."

"Yes, sir."

"Do you know how hard I work to get Honor Barracks?"

"No, sir."

"Stand at attention when I talk to you."

"Yes, sir." Billy straightened and the lieutenant moved closer to him.

"Roarke, if I ever find out that your little escapes stopped me from becoming battalion commander, I will get you and I will get you good. Do you understand that?"

"Yes, sir."

"Get in there and start scrubbing."

Billy picked up the cleaning materials and carried them into the barracks. He sat in the middle of the area stained by the pickle juice and shook the cleanser can all around him. He dipped the brush into the water and scrubbed.

Something surprised Billy. As he sat there, in the beginning of a task that would not end until morning, he noticed something peculiar. He wasn't afraid. The more Lieutenant Mitchell scolded him, and even threatened him, the less it scared him. He had seen his barracks leader scared himself, by a boy just a couple of years older than him. Lieutenant Mitchell did not scare Billy, because Billy did not respect or care about Lieutenant Mitchell. What his barracks leader thought about him did not matter. So much had happened to Billy that he no longer had the energy to be frightened by everything that was thrown his way, by everyone who yelled at him, threatened him, hated him. So, he saved his fear. He saved it for when he would need it.

Mitchell had arranged for cadets to watch Billy for one hour at a time. They were ordered not to let him rest. The barracks leader made sure not to include any of Billy's friends on the schedule he made, for fear that they would not make him work.

Billy's pace greatly slowed after an hour. His arms, back and neck ached. His fingers hurt so much he had to constantly switch the hands working the brush. His underwear – all that he wore, along with a T-shirt – was soaked with soapy water. He was becoming sleepy.

At times his guards would themselves fall asleep, and Billy took those opportunities to stop working. He'd watch them with narrow, tired eyes and start scrubbing once they woke up.

After four cadets came Corporal Roberts. Roberts was the first to harass Billy beyond telling him to keep working. Roberts, at first, appeared tired like all the rest, but soon became alert at the prospect of playing taskmaster.

"Move it, Roarke," he said as he sat on the floor outside the growing circle of wetness. "Scrub harder." Roberts poured more cleanser on the floor. "Scrub, scrub, scrub."

Billy couldn't move faster. His fingers were stuck in the mold of his grip on the brush. The pain seemed the only thing that kept him awake, but he wanted to sleep now more than he ever wanted to eat good food. His head would drop in sleep, even as he pushed the brush, but Roberts was there to wake him with a slap on the head.

But Roberts didn't last long himself. After about fifteen minutes he laid his head on the pillow he brought and fell asleep. Billy didn't have the energy to think about strategy. He simply did what his body demanded. With his hand still on the brush, he dropped his head onto the wet floor and fell asleep.

It was two-twenty in the morning and Billy Roarke was asleep in a pool of soapy water in the middle of Barracks C.

The reveille bugle blew the boys awake. Billy and Roberts sat up and looked groggily at each other. Billy wiped the wetness from his face and mouth as Mitchell approached them.

"Why are *you* here, Roberts? You're not last on the list."

Roberts stood slowly, allowing himself some time to think. "I . . . I wanted to finish the job, sir. I watched him the whole time since I came on duty."

Mitchell looked at Billy. "Shower up, Roarke. You look disgusting."

Billy walked to his bunk and took a cake of soap and a towel from his footlocker. Gilbert put a hand on his wet shoulder. "Are you okay, pal?"

He didn't answer him.

Billy learned one thing that night. Maybe Lieutenant Mitchell didn't scare him anymore, but his barracks leader – and others like him – still had the power to make his life difficult. Difficult, and very unpleasant.

CHAPTER
Twenty-four

Mrs. Roarke looked pretty Saturday morning. She sat in the bleachers near the reviewing stand of the parade ground with a smile that awaited something wonderful. Her light blue dress with white polka dots, like a mirror, matched the spring sky: a blue plane flecked with clean white clouds. Her white hat and gloves made vibrant the colors of her skin, hair and eyes. Mrs. Roarke was a beautiful woman when her mind was not burdened.

She heard music, turned her head and stretched her neck to view the corps of cadets entering the parade ground. The formal structure and precision of young boys marching made her proud that her son was part of this pageantry.

Her smile grew as each company passed, leading to the last one, Company D, the one with her son, Private Billy Roarke.

Her eyes moved quickly from one cadet to the next, but she was not able to find him. Too many boys, moving too fast. Whenever Company D marched back into closer view she studied them more carefully. But the boys were wearing their dress hats with wide brims, and that made them difficult to identify.

When the cadets engaged in "Pass in Review" they would all turn their faces toward the reviewing stand. That would give her a good look at each of them. She would see him then.

Lieutenant Mitchell ordered, "Eyes right," and Company D passed the stand. Mrs. Roarke saw each boy's face. She did not see Billy. He wasn't there.

Her face reclaimed the familiar look of concern she had often worn the last two years. Where was her son? She thought of reasons why he was not in the parade, and the one she hoped for was that he was sick. It had come to this, hoping that her son was sick. She felt ashamed for thinking such a thing, but was fearful of worse. Worse had happened before.

During the parade, Billy sat alone in an unused classroom. Lieutenant Mitchell had ordered him there without consulting the commandant. There was nothing in the room but one chair, and Billy sat in it. He was tired from last night, but couldn't sleep. The chair was too hard. He just sat with his arms folded across his chest, looking at nothing, thinking about his mother.

Major Chandler saw Mrs. Roarke alone in his office. He apologized profusely for not informing her of the situation. He explained that he had tried calling home once last night, but couldn't get through, and that the events surrounding Parents' Day kept him occupied after that. He assured her that he was unaware of Billy not participating in the parade and that Lieutenant Mitchell had not followed procedure in confining him to the classroom. All that aside, Major Chandler told Mrs. Roarke that he accepted complete responsibility for her coming to the parade without knowing about her son.

Mrs. Roarke was distressed. She spoke with frequent pauses designed to help compose herself. She told Major Chandler that she appreciated his apology, but that the ultimate responsibility was with her son. She told him that she was unable that day to meet with Billy, that she was too upset.

The major agreed, adding that he himself needed more time to further investigate the incident before deciding on a course of action.

Together they decided to wait three days. On Tuesday afternoon the three of them would meet to discuss Billy – and his future at Eagleton Military Academy for Boys.

Billy reported to Major Chandler's office. His mother was seated in front of the commandant's desk and gave him a quick look with no greeting.

"Sit down, Private Roarke," the commandant said.

"Yes, sir." Billy sat down next to his mother, looked at her, but said nothing. Mrs. Roarke's eyes remained on the major.

"Private Roarke," the commandant began, "let me begin by stating that I'm not sure you understand the seriousness of leaving this campus, of going AWOL . . ."

"I do sir."

"Please do not interrupt me, Private."

"Yes, sir."

"I understand you considered this breach of code to be punishable by K.P. duty. Is that correct?"

"Uhm, yes, sir. I did."

"Well, I'm afraid it's much more serious than that."

"Yes, sir."

"In the first place, we here at Eagleton are fully responsible for our cadets. If one of them decides to leave campus, we then have no control over their safety. Anything could happen and we wouldn't be able to respond. Do you understand that?"

"Yes, sir."

The major motioned toward Mrs. Roarke. "Your mother, Private, placed your well-being in our hands. It is a poor reflection on us if we do not honor our commitment to her."

"Yes, sir."

His mother sat stiff and still. She did not appear to have moved an inch since Billy entered the office.

"Now," he continued, "I understand that you left campus in order to acquire some food from the market down the street. Is that correct?"

"Yes, sir."

"Can you tell me why?"

"I was hungry, sir."

On hearing this, his mother took a breath and raised her shoulders even higher. She turned her head and gave Billy a stern look.

"Hungry?" the commandant replied. "Do we not give you three square meals a day, and request that you eat everything on your tray?"

"Yes, sir. I just didn't like the food."

"You didn't like the food."

"Yes, sir."

The major sighed. "Private Roarke, are you even mildly aware of the sacrifices our nation is making at this moment?"

"Yes, sir."

"Well, that's a strange way of showing it, is it not?"

"Yes, sir."

Mrs. Roarke continued to look at the commandant, again not moving, but still showing tremendous strain in her upright body.

"There are people right here at Eagleton, Private, people who have sacrificed greatly for this war."

"Yes, sir."

"They've had to endure things that most of us cannot imagine. And yet you felt it necessary to leave campus, to go Absent Without Leave, in order to gather up some food for yourself."

"Yes, sir."

"I find that very selfish, young man, very selfish."

"Yes, sir."

At this the commandant paused, sat back in his chair and observed Billy, who was seated with his hands folded between his legs, his head bent down.

Major Chandler sat upright again and continued. "I will tell you, Private, that you have a couple of supporters here at school."

"Sir?"

"Corporal Gilbert came in to see me. He told me that he deserved whatever punishment you receive because he ate some of the food."

Billy lifted his head. "He did, sir?"

"Yes, but I didn't buy it. Corporal Gilbert did not leave this campus and he will not be punished. I admire his honor."

"Yes, sir. Corporal Gilbert . . . uhm, in fact, tried to talk me out of going AWOL."

Major Chandler nodded, then spoke. "Someone else came to your defense."

"Yes, sir?"

"Mr. Hollenbeck."

"The Colonel, sir?"

"Yes, Private Roarke, Mr. Hollenbeck. Why does that surprise you?"

"Uh, well, uhm . . . I didn't think he liked me, sir."

"Well, Private, as a matter of fact, Mr. Hollenbeck spoke very highly of you, and of what he perceives as your unusually strong character. I have never heard him speak of a cadet in such terms."

Billy looked puzzled. "He did, sir?"

"Yes, he did."

Mrs. Roarke's posture remained, and though Billy gave her a quick glance, she did not look back at him.

"Now then," Major Chandler said, "the punishment for such a breach, Private, the punishment for going Absent Without Leave is not, as you thought, K.P. duty."

"Yes, sir."

"The punishment, Private Roarke, is expulsion."

Billy lowered his head. His mother closed her eyes.

"However, I have lived long enough and seen enough to know that not all situations merit the same response. You will be punished, Private, punished severely, but you will not be expelled."

His mother released a breath which seemed to deflate her body. Her shoulders dropped and her back curved in deep relief. Her eyes remained closed and her lips barely moved to a silent, "Thank you."

Billy cried. He removed a handkerchief from his pants pocket, wiped his tears and blew his nose.

Major Chandler paused, allowing the boy to recover his emotions, then continued. "I will tell you, however, Private Roarke, that this is your final chance. There will be no mercy from me should this ever occur again. You must promise me that you will never leave this campus again."

"I promise, Major. I've learned my lesson. I'm sorry. I won't ever leave again."

"Very well, Private. We will discuss your punishment at a later time. As for now, you are dismissed." Major Chandler stood and bowed his head. "Mrs. Roarke."

"Thank you, Major," she said as she stood to grasp his hand. "Thank you."

Billy and his mother left the office and stood facing each other in the courtyard.

"Look at me," she said.

"Yes, Mom?"

She bent forward to directly deliver her words. "I never told you how I felt after you beat that boy." Billy's eyes swung down. "Look at me," she ordered. His eyes obeyed.

"*My heart was ripped in two.*" She stressed each word as she spoke in a tone that Billy had never heard before. "I had an ache in my heart that I had never felt. It felt like nothing, like *nothing*, I've ever felt."

Billy's lips quivered, but his eyes remained on his mother's face. He stood with his hands folded on his belt buckle.

"My parents are dead. I've been without my husband for two years. And yet nothing has felt like what hit me right here." She tapped the middle of her chest with a fist.

"Maybe I'm just bad, Mom."

Mrs. Roarke snapped. "How dare you! How dare you try to avoid responsibility for what you did! You did that yourself, and don't you ever try to pretend that you couldn't help it because you are bad! Do you understand me?"

"Yes, Mom."

"I've got one more thing to tell you, and you better listen very well." She stood straight up, then bent forward again. "This was your last chance. Do you understand that?"

"Yes, Mom."

"This is it. If I am ever called to school again to deal with your behavior, you, young man, will pray unceasingly to the Lord God Almighty to save you from the hell that your life will become. Is that clear?"

"Yes, Mom."

"It's over, Billy. I've had enough. I can't take this anymore."

Mrs. Roarke straightened her back and turned to leave.

"Bye, Mom," he said softly.

She said nothing. Billy watched her as she walked away, down the corridor, out the front gate and into a waiting cab, never looking back at her son.

CHAPTER
Twenty-five

Billy was placed on probation. For the remainder of the year any significant offense would result in his permanent expulsion from Eagleton. This school year was almost over, but where he would go next year would become a real problem if he were expelled.

In addition, Billy was put to work. He was given no demerits, no light K.P. duty with Mr. Leonard, no marching tours on the drill field. He was made to work. Each day during recess and free time he reported to the office to receive his orders, which consisted of whatever the school needed done. He scrubbed large, smelly trash cans. He pulled weeds in the courtyard garden. He washed dishes. Mopped floors. Dug big holes for any reason big holes were needed. For one hour each school day, Billy worked hard. Hard like a man who got paid to work hard.

There was more. Mrs. Roarke called the school Friday morning to notify them that Billy would not be coming home that weekend. As a result, Major Chandler left strict orders that the boy would not be working or serving any punishment during the weekend.

The weekend was boring. There was lots of free time and not many things to do. Billy's friends had gone home, so he spent much of the time lying on his bunk with a book.

The next week his mother called again to say that Billy would not be coming home. When Major Chandler learned of this, he phoned Mrs. Roarke and talked to her for some time about Billy and his situation.

He did go home that weekend to find his mother acting without any apparent anger toward him. She never mentioned anything about his problems at school, and though she rarely laughed or smiled, seemed happy to have him home. Billy was relieved. These days his mother's moods largely determined his own.

On Sunday after church, Mrs. Roarke invited Charlie and Randall to join them for a picnic at the park. The boys played ball while she read the paper. The news from the war was good. The Allies were ready to take Rome, the first capital city to fall from the Nazis. The Allies were winning the war.

The next day at school, Lieutenant Mitchell spoke to Billy for the first time since he confined him to the empty classroom. He told him to mop the latrine during barracks cleanup. He was not harsh in his command; it was an ordinary order, unusual only in its distance from his previous command.

Major Chandler had spoken to the barracks leader about the qualities of leadership and the importance of not extracting revenge from subordinates. Lieutenant Mitchell appeared to respond to the major's words.

Before lights out that night, Billy and Gilbert lay in their bunks and talked of the summer.

"Hey, Roarke, how'd you like to come over to my house when school's out? I'll have our cook make you anything you want."

"That'd be swell. I could ride my bike."

"You bet. And we can ride our bikes together around town. Maybe go to the Rose Bowl and explore the canyons around there."

"That sounds fun."

"It's going to be a great summer, Roarke."

"Yeah. I can't wait."

The bugle blew taps and the barracks lights went out.

"Goodnight, Roarke."

"Goodnight, Gilbert. Dream about the summer for me."

"My pleasure, pal. It's going to be a good one."

A loud radio woke Billy the next morning shortly before reveille. A roll call of French towns brought him slowly out of his sleep. Le Havre, Abbeville, Dieppe, Caen, Amiens, Cherbourg. He lifted his upper body with an arm and heard clearly the radio's voice: "Once again, America, let me repeat. Under the command of General Eisenhower, Allied naval forces supported by strong air forces began landing Allied armies this morning on the northern coast of France."

D-Day. Billy slowly left his bed and kneeled at the side of his bunk, his elbows resting on the rail while his head rested on pressed hands. While the barracks celebrated, he knelt and prayed for his father. He knew he was there.

He went to the kitchen after breakfast. "Mr. Leonard. It happened. D-Day."

Mr. Leonard looked up from the sink where he was scrubbing a pan. He smiled. "D-Day, Billy. God bless General Ike."

"Is your son there, you think?"

"No, Billy. My boy's still in the States. What about your daddy?"

"I'm sure he's there."

Mr. Leonard dried his hands. "I'll pray fo' him. God bless you, boy."

Study hall was cancelled that evening. The entire school gathered in the auditorium after dinner to listen to the radio broadcast of President Roosevelt's prayer to the nation.

The corps of cadets was silent as they listened to the words of the president. But even the breathing seemed to stop midway through as he said, "Some will never return. Embrace these, Father, and receive them, Thy heroic servants, into Thy kingdom."

Major Chandler addressed the cadets after the broadcast. He spoke of sacrifice and honor, and of the heroism of young soldiers delivering the world from the evils of tyranny. "Honor these men with your memory and your hearts, cadets of Eagleton. Never forget what they have done, never diminish their great deed, and never forget that nations do not survive without men such as these."

That day nations prayed while their sons fought, killed and died. D-Day brought fury to the battlefield and holiness to the homefront. Billy lay in bed that night, praying until he fell asleep. His father was fighting a war.

CHAPTER
Twenty-six

The next afternoon, while the junior school had recess, Billy helped Coach Riley clean out the equipment shed.

Before dinner he stood near his bunk, drying off from a shower, as Hazelnut approached him.

"Oh, sorry about your ball, Roarke."

"What do you mean?"

"Didn't Gilbert tell you? We needed a baseball for our game and he said you had one, so we took it from your footlocker."

"Where is it?"

"We lost it. I hit a homer over the fence. A real beauty, boy. Could've cleared Ebbets Field for sure."

"You lost my ball? How could you lose my ball? How could you . . ."

"Hey, relax, Roarke. It's just a dumb baseball."

Billy sat on his bunk and thought for a moment, then he asked, "Where exactly is the ball?"

"I hit it over the left field fence. I don't know exactly where it is. It hit some trees and fell to the ground. But you can't get it, Roarke. It's out of bounds. There's no way you can get caught bein' AWOL again. You know that. Just relax. It's just a ball."

That night, after lights out, Billy lay on his back in his bunk, staring at the black above him, waiting for a time when he thought everyone would be asleep. He didn't know how much time had passed, but it had seemed a long while since he last heard the movements of boys positioning themselves for a comfortable sleep. He slowly rose from his bunk, trying to avoid the usual chorus from the bed springs. He was unsuccessful. His departure created, what seemed to him, crashing cymbals amidst the silence of night. He stood motionless, waiting for the sounds of awakened boys, but heard none. He then turned to the task of putting on his shoes. He kept his pajamas on and ignored the need for socks.

Billy walked lightly through the latrine and out the door. He looked left, then right, saw no one and started walking with increasing swiftness to the athletic field.

The moon lit the field with an almost daytime brightness, but the trees beyond the fence would shield much of the light, making it difficult for Billy to find the ball. He approached the left field side of the seven-foot-high, chain-link fence and started to climb. His hands grabbed hard, thin metal. He lifted himself higher, while his feet pushed against the stiff fence for support. He had to jump off the fence and start again several times. The task was proving difficult. He couldn't fit his shoes between the holes created by the chain link. His arms were tiring and his fingers were hurting. He stopped to rest, standing before the fence and thinking about what he needed to do. He couldn't let a silly old fence stand in his way, he thought. He tried again with increased vigor and an audible, "C'mon, Billy," and made it to the top.

As he tried to send his right leg over to the other side, he felt a tug on the back of his pajama top.

"Let's go, Roarke."

"Lieutenant Mitchell."

"That's right, Roarke. We thought we cured you of your wandering ways. Out for a midnight snack?"

"No, sir. I had to look for my ball," he replied as he remained perched atop the fence.

The lieutenant laughed. "You had to look for your ball? At ten o'clock at night you had to look for your ball? Roarke, are you stable? Get down from the fence, Roarke. We've got a late-night meeting with the commandant."

Billy jumped back onto school soil and was promptly escorted to Major Chandler's office. He sat and waited while Mitchell informed the commandant of Billy's latest excursion.

After about ten minutes, Major Chandler entered the office wearing a bathrobe and slippers. He seated himself behind his desk, ordered Mitchell to leave, and stared at Billy. The major scooted his chair closer to his desk, put his hands together on the desktop, forming a triangle with his arms and chest, and spoke.

"Private Roarke, what in heaven's name caused you to once again leave this school? I thought you had given me your word that there would be no more of these shenanigans. I am deeply upset, and I feel deeply betrayed. I thought I saw something in you, Roarke. I trusted you. I believed you to be a young man of honesty and integrity. You sat right there in that same chair where you're sitting now and promised me, promised me, Roarke, that you would never try to leave this school again. Your mother is going to be very disappointed. You know this means expulsion. And what will she do with you now? You've already been booted from your public school. I am very hurt, young man, very hurt."

The commandant paused, but Billy said nothing.

"Well, what have you got to say for yourself now?"

Billy was calm. "I had to find my ball, sir."

"Your ball? What in heaven's name are you talking about, Roarke?"

"The fellas in my barracks needed a baseball for their game, so they took mine without asking. And then one of them hit it over the fence. I was afraid one of the neighborhood kids was going to pick it up. I had to get it."

"Private Roarke, you are making no sense to me. You would risk expulsion? You would go back on your promise to me and your mother for an insignificant baseball?"

"It's not insignificant, sir."

"What do you mean, Roarke? You could have bought a baseball during your weekend leave."

"Not that baseball, sir."

"And what, pray tell, is so special about *that* baseball?"

"My father gave it to me, sir. It was the last thing he gave me before he left."

Major Chandler took a deep breath, sat back in his chair and rubbed his chin. He kept his hand on his face and stared at his desk. Billy sat quietly, his eyes on the commandant, who did not respond for a long time.

Finally he looked up and asked, "Where's your father, son?"

"I'm pretty sure he just landed in Normandy, sir."

Major Chandler said nothing for a few moments.

"When was the last time you saw your father?"

"Last summer, when he was on leave before shipping out to England. But he's been away from our family for about two years."

"Your dad likes baseball?"

Billy smiled. "Yes, sir. The Brooklyn Dodgers, sir."

"I'm a Cardinals man myself, Roarke."

"Yes, sir. Stan Musial, sir."

Major Chandler sat back in his chair. "Roarke, my father would take me to ball games, way back around the 1890s. It was a different game back then, but my dad and I loved baseball, too."

"Is your dad alive, sir?"

"Oh, heavens no. I'm an old man, Roarke. My father died about twenty years ago. But, uh, say, so you say your dad gave you that ball before he left?"

"Yes, sir."

"Mitchell!" Major Chandler yelled into the next room. "Get in here."

Lieutenant Mitchell entered the office. "Yes, sir."

"Mitchell, secure a flashlight and get back here. We've got a baseball to find."

"Sir?"

"A baseball, Mitchell! A baseball! Now hop to it!"

"Yes, sir . . . um, yes, sir."

Twenty-seven

There was no drilling the last week of school. There were no inspections. Eagleton gradually released its students into the stream of civilian life rather than plunging them stone cold back into their natural world.

There was no study hall the last week of school, but Mr. Kooler came by to visit and to wish the boys the best of summers.

The Colonel was the only element in Eagleton which acted as if school were not ending. Up to the last day, he taught as he always had. Only at the end of his last session with the class, on Friday before lunch, did the Colonel acknowledge the end.

He stood before them. "As you know, this marks the end of my tenure as your teacher. You will all be passed to the eighth grade, but that is no achievement. That is a superficial promotion.

"My task was to toughen your mind. To teach you to think under duress. Nothing of worth is achieved in comfort. Had I created this classroom in the image of a playground, I would have cheated you and made hollow any success you believed to achieve. That success would never be duplicated in the world outside these walls.

"I look forward to hearing of your achievements in the years ahead. Leave this classroom and do great things. Dismissed."

Billy left the Colonel's classroom, and in the afternoon he left Eagleton. He went home.

*****

Billy turned thirteen in July, and his mother had a party for him at their house. Gilbert, Hazelnut and Maglioni came. Randall and Charlie were there.

It was strange for Billy to have his military school friends at his house. He had only seen them before at Eagleton, and it was strange for him to witness the mingling of his two sets of friends.

Charlie liked Billy's other friends. Randall hated them. He stood alone with Billy in the backyard while Mrs. Roarke led the other boys in a game of "Pin the Tail on the Donkey."

"I guess they do have girls at that Eagleson joint, huh, Billy?"

"Lay off, Randall."

"And what's with that dopey brainy kid? I can't believe you'd be pals with a dope like that."

"Gilbert's a great guy. If you don't like my friends, you can go home."

Randall took a step backward and raised his hands. "Woah. Take it easy, pal. I was just makin' observations. Listen, don't forget your first friends, Billy. We're your real pals. Charlie 'n' me."

"I'm not forgetting anybody, but I've got other friends now, too. A lot of things happened at military school, and these guys were good pals to me, especially Gilbert."

"What happened? How come you don't talk about it?"

"I'll tell you all about it someday. I've just wanted to enjoy the summer and think about being home."

The next morning after church, Billy sat on the sofa reading while his mother stood by the window. "Billy, sweetheart," she said, "it's lovely today. Why don't you go outside and play with your friends?"

"Uhm, I feel like finishing this book, Mom. I'll go out later."

"All right, dear." As she was leaving her place by the window, Mrs. Roarke saw a teenage boy in a messenger's uniform drop his bike on their front yard and stride up the walkway with a telegram in his hand.

"Billy," she said in a quick voice, "go to your room."

"Why, Mom? What's the matter?"

"Go, Billy. Go now."

He left the sofa, leaving his book, and walked down the hall to his room with his face turned back toward the parlor, looking for the object of his mother's concern.

He heard the knock after entering his room. He closed the bedroom door and stood with his ear to it, trying to decipher the distant sounds. Billy heard the messenger enter the house. He then heard a quiet voice speaking, but did not hear his mother. He still did not hear her, even though it was clear the boy was now leaving.

The front door closed and there was now silence. Billy was afraid to come out, but he heard his mother's quick steps down the hall and opened his door. Mrs. Roarke turned her

face from him, quickly entered her bedroom and locked herself in. He rushed to her door.

"Mom?" Billy knocked. "Mom? Let me in, please." He
heard crying, the sound muffled by pillows. He knocked
again. "Mom, please let me in. Please, Mom, please."

His mother did not reply. Billy cried as he slowly dropped
to the floor, leaning against the door. "Mom, let me in.
Mom!"

He heard no answer and no movement from inside his
mother's room. He stopped knocking and he stopped calling
for her, but he did not leave. He sat alone and cried alone for
a very long time.

At last, his mother opened the door. Her face was battered
by tears, but she was no longer crying. She lifted Billy from
the floor and led him to her bed, where she sat and held her
crying son.

Billy's father was buried in France. Buried alongside other
young men and boys from California, from Texas, from
Canada, from England. Buried in dirt far from his home. Far
from his family.

There was a short article in the Pasadena paper about Lieutenant Roarke. He had died on D-Day.

During the next week many people came to the Roarke's
house to pay their respects. They would sit with his mother in
the parlor and speak in unnaturally soft voices. Billy would
come out to say hello and then gradually make his way to his
bedroom, where he stayed until they left.

There was a memorial service for his father, which nearly
filled the church. Billy's grandparents had come from Oregon. His friends and their families were there. So was Mrs.
Pearson, Major Chandler, Mr. Kooler and the Colonel.

During this time Billy and his mother, who was given time off from work, did not speak much, but they stayed close to each another. They sat in the parlor and listened to the radio, and Billy would always sit at the kitchen table when his mother prepared meals.

He spent much of the time thinking about his father. Most of all, he wished he could talk to him, just one more time.

CHAPTER
Twenty-eight

Two weeks after the service, Billy and Gilbert rode their bikes down Huntington Drive. They rode until the grid of street blocks turned into a grid of orange groves.

They stopped at a stand that offered all the orange juice they could drink for ten cents. They took their Dixie cups of juice and sat against the side of the stand.

"Boy, Roarke, this is the farthest I've ever come this way on my bike."

"Yeah, me, too."

Gilbert finished his juice. "This is good. You want a refill yet?"

"No, not yet."

Gilbert got up to get more juice. When he returned he took a long sip before carefully sitting down again, so as not to spill his drink. "Boy, this sure is good. They didn't have anything that tasted like this at Eagleton, did they?"

"No."

"Are you coming back to school next year, Roarke?"

Billy took a sip, then spoke. "Yeah, I think so. I didn't get kicked out."

"Well, I'm glad you're coming back. It was really swell to have you there."

"Thanks." He looked at Gilbert. "How was your summer camp?"

"Kind of like Eagleton, except instead of marching and sitting in class they made you hike and make Indian crafts."

"Hmm."

"Yeah . . . uhm, gee, Roarke." Gilbert paused before continuing. "I didn't get a chance to tell you at the memorial, but I'm awful sorry about your father."

Billy looked into his cup of juice. "Thanks, Gilbert. I'm all right."

"You know, I told my mother this. Your father must have been a great guy, because you're the swellest guy I know."

"Thanks. But I'm not good like my dad."

"Aw, sure you are. You're always hard on yourself, Roarke. Besides, you're really still just a kid."

"I never told you, Gilbert, why I was sent to Eagleton."

"I know, partner. You don't have to tell me."

Billy finished his juice, then flung the remaining drops from his cup. He stared straight ahead as he spoke. "I beat up a kid in my class real bad. I beat him up because he was German and his dad wasn't in the war. I beat him up so bad an ambulance came and took him to the hospital." Billy turned his face to Gilbert. "Do you still think I'm the swellest kid you know?"

"Well . . ." Gilbert paused. "It's like what Mr. Kooler said that one night to you. It's not possible to be perfect. I'm sure you were sorry about it."

"Yeah. Sure."

"Listen, Roarke. Do you think your father would want you thinking you're a horrible guy?"

Billy looked at Gilbert. "No."

"Then make him happy. If he's looking down on you, make him happy. Let him know he made a great son."

"I can't be good like he was, Gilbert. I can't take his place."

"I don't think you're supposed to take his place. But you know what, Roarke?" Gilbert put a hand on Billy's shoulder. "You're still the swellest guy I know."

The next day, Billy stood at the doorstep with a confidence that surprised him. He knocked and waited for the man to open the door.

"Yes?" the man said. "Oh, young man, Thomas isn't here. He's at his grandparents' for a week. If you'll give me your name, I'll tell him you called on him."

"I'm Billy Roarke."

The man's eyes grew and he began to shut the door.

"Please, Mr. Mueller. I came here to apologize to you and your family. I've been away at military school. I'm out now, and I wanted to apologize face to face."

He left the door open. "Well?"

"I don't blame you for being angry, sir. I understand that." Billy's confidence was now staggering a bit under the sober eye of Mr. Mueller. "Uh, is Thomas doing all right?"

"Yes, Thomas is doing fine," he replied in a business-like tone.

"All I can say, sir, is that I'm awful sorry for what I did. I used to be sorry because it got me in trouble, because I had to go to military school for it. Now, I have to tell you, I'm sorry for hurting your son and your family. I'm just awful sorry, sir."

Mr. Mueller's stare softened. "Well . . . if you'd like, you may come by next week to talk to Thomas. He'll be coming home this Sunday."

"Thank you, Mr. Mueller. I'll do that."

When his mother came home, Billy told her what he had done that afternoon.

"That's wonderful, dear," she said.

"Mom? Am I going back to military school next year?"

"No, Billy. I found a private school that you can walk to. You'll be living at home."

"Thank you, Mom. You're not going to have any more trouble from me; I promise."

Mrs. Roarke smiled. "We'll see about that."

"Mom?"

"Yes?"

"We're gonna be okay, right? You and me?"

"Yes, dear. We're going to be fine."

"Even though we miss Dad?"

"We'll always miss him, Billy."

He lunged forward and hugged his mother. They held each other for a long moment.

"Billy?"

"Yes, Mom?"

"How about treating your mother to a chocolate soda?"

"Swell!" Billy broke from his mother's embrace and ran toward his room. "I'm just gonna get my money."

When he reached the hallway he stopped, turned and looked at his mother. "Mom, I'm going to take care of you."

"We're going to take care of each other," she said.

Billy and his mother started on their way to Himmelfarb's. The flag in the window gave a quick flutter as Mrs. Roarke firmly shut the front door, the gold star reflecting the light from a clear, sunny day.

The End

www.briankaradashianbooks.com
www.facebook.com/AFlagintheWindow

Author Biography

Brian Karadashian teaches elementary school in the Rancho Bernardo community of San Diego. He received a B.A. from San Diego State University in 1983 and an M.A. from Stanford University in 1990. He has had articles published in the Los Angeles *Herald-Examiner* and the Dallas *Times Herald*. He has two grown stepchildren, Erik and Samantha, and lives with his wife, Marcia, in Escondido, California. *A Flag in the Window* is his first novel.

Artist Biography

Richard DeRosset is a maritime and aviation historian. He is the official artist for the San Diego Maritime Museum and is an official U.S. Coast Guard artist. His paintings are displayed worldwide, including at the Central Military Museum in Moscow and at the Smithsonian Institution. His work can be viewed at richardderosset.com.

CPSIA information can be obtained at www.ICGtesting.com
Printed in the USA
LVOW120109230313

325679LV00001BA/1/P